I0610599

PETE CLEMENTS

THE LATITUDE

Black Rose Writing | Texas

©2019, 2020, 2023 by Pete Clements
All rights reserved. No part of this book may be reproduced, stored in a retrieval system or transmitted in any form or by any means without the prior written permission of the publishers, except by a reviewer who may quote brief passages in a review to be printed in a newspaper, magazine or journal.

The author grants the final approval for this literary material.

Second printing

This is a work of fiction. Names, characters, businesses, places, events, and incidents are either the products of the author's imagination or used in a fictitious manner. Any resemblance to actual persons, living or dead, or actual events is purely coincidental.

ISBN: 978-1-68433-396-7 (Paperback); 978-1-94471-570-0 (Hardcover)
PUBLISHED BY BLACK ROSE WRITING
www.blackrosewriting.com

Printed in the United States of America
Suggested Retail Price (SRP) $17.95 (Paperback); $22.95 (Hardcover)

The Latitude is printed in Baskerville

*The final word count for this book may not match your standard expectation versus the final page count. In an effort to reduce paper usage and energy costs, Black Rose Writing, as a planet-friendly publisher, does its best to eliminate unnecessary waste without lessening your reading experience.

She had him with her naked eyes, as he pulled the cord. *Show me your colors, Sky King*, she thought.

THE LATITUDE

CHAPTER ONE
WHERE CITRUS IS KING

"Quiet, please! On the air! On the air! Quiet, please!"

As the sign above the soundproof door of the NBC, New York, TV Studio 1A quit flashing, the red light popped on.

The news of his leap to fame spread not only locally but to social media, Internet blogs, and even the networks. It happened on June 5, fourteen months earlier, and now he was on TV.

Music came up, and show titles rolled. His face appeared in a close-up on the monitor. As directed, he looked straight at the lens. His name was supered under his face, and the camera slowly dollied out to reveal a typical talk-show set in earth tones. A director's chair sat stage right, or left to the viewer, with a small desk opposite for the host.

The director pointed at him.

"I am...I was...a skydiving instructor," he said slowly, still unable to believe what happened even after telling the story so many times. "I arched out of the plane, a Cessna 182, at 6,000 feet, my head back, arms up and out, back arched, and legs cocked at the knees—free-fall mode. At 2,500, I pulled the ripcord. The canopy came out in a rod-stiff ball, caught in its own suspension lines—a streamer malfunction. After I got past the shock, feeling seconds howling past, I pulled the reserve chute. It streamed out the same way. Then I ran out of time."

"And he's alive to tell us about it!" the host said on cue. "Right here! Welcome to *A.M. America* on NBC! I'm Ted Osgood. Here with me with his terrifying tale, a headline story heard 'round the world, from Darien Connecticut—and it's been a long wait—is Bill Burton!"

The floor director smiled at him wide-eyed, nodding violently for him to reply.

He tried to smile at the camera. "Good morning. Sorry I took so long."

"Tell the folks, Bill, what exactly took so long—hospitals and whatnot, right?"

"About four months in lots of hospitals, then about ten months in whatnot—physical therapy."

"You look great. Steel plate somewhere?"

He tried to forget the pain, the months of agonizing over it. He packed dozens of chutes, and none of them failed. Why his? Part of him didn't believe it happened, but it did, so where had he gone wrong? He was a pro. How could he have made such a mistake with both chutes?

Burning deep inside was a frightening feeling he didn't want to acknowledge, so he shoved it away. *If I didn't make a mistake, that means it wasn't an accident.*

"A steel plate in my head, fused lumbar vertebrae, a shattered pelvis with a steel pin. Pins in each leg, which were broken in the fall, then rebroken several times in surgery. I'll wear a little black rubber wedge in my shoe for life, because they couldn't quite make my legs the same length. That's it."

"That's enough!" Ted said in amazement. "A big price to make you a star, my friend. Good picture, by the way, in the glossies. Let me get this straight. You jumped from over a mile up."

"Right." He remembered how the ground looked, when he thought everything was normal.

"The parachute doesn't open."

"Right." His first twinge of panic hit when he saw the fowled lines. Then real dread struck when the reserve failed.

"Man, how does *that* feel?"

There was no way he could explain. Man can't fly unassisted. He'd lectured students on chute safety repeatedly. If your chute fails...

Blotchy, whirling glimpses rushed before his eyes. A roaring wall of wind ripping his mouth open, the goggles shoving against his eyes, his arms groping against the lines during those final seconds, but they were as taut as vibrating piano wire. Then pain struck like an orange canopy of molten lava, the cone of a tornado, white light exploding, crashing through window glass...then nothing.

The director pointed at his mouth, indicating he should say something. With sweat breaking out on his back, all he could think of was falling.

Ted Osgood waited a second, then covered for his guest. "You fall, not on a pillow or a haystack, but on blacktop."

"The runway at the airport," he managed to say.

"And you set some kind of world record for this?"

"I lived. Nobody who ever jumped from that altitude ever did before. I hold the world's record."

"Got any plans for the future?"

"I don't know."

"Are you done with skydiving?"

"I don't know. I was an experienced instructor and dive master. I miss it."

"Who packs the parachutes?"

He didn't like the question, but he said, "The skydiver's responsible for his own equipment." *Did I do it wrong somehow? If not me, then who?* he wondered for the thousandth time.

Music came up again. They were out of time. The floor director made whirly-bird signals with his hand to wind things up.

Ted turned to the camera. "An amazing story of terror, pain, determination, and a miracle—Lady Luck where no one has been before. Thanks for sharing it with us, Bill Burton." He reached over to shake Bill's hand.

"We'll be right back," he told the camera.

*   *   *

Bill was out of the studio and down the elevator before the commercial hit the nation's living rooms. Back on the street, he felt like a spent stage actor, long after curtain call, late leaving the theater when the stage worshippers are all gone and the play over. Nobody cared about the star at that point. It was back to reality.

He realized he had absolutely nowhere to go, not in an hour or a week. He wandered into Charlie O's, a bar on 48th Street too early for lunch, but he couldn't face a train ride yet.

Darien, Bill thought, thinking of his town. *Jesus.*

He ordered a draft. A couple early birds were scattered along the bar, guys in suits privately contemplating their martinis, along with a problem or a plan. He didn't think he had a problem, except he didn't have a plan.

At least he hadn't been disfigured. He could walk and looked OK for somebody twenty-one-years old. The bartender didn't ask him for ID. What was left of his body had never been in better shape.

Something would come up. He knew it. He just wished he knew how and why it happened.

He cabbed to Grand Central and got on the commuter train for Darien.

★   ★   ★

In the days after the TV interview, Bill wandered the town aimlessly. Old friends expressed sincere pleasure at his recovery. Friends of his parents asked where he was going to college, so they could tell him about the soaring success of their offspring, all in business administration, medicine, or law.

He drove Mom's car to the airport and stopped at Skydive, Incorporated, his former employer, saw the old boss and the kids in the office, asked a few innocent questions while trying to act casual and kept his eyes and ears open for any odd remark, implication, or innuendo.

The Skydive crew seemed glad to see him, though the boss was understandably distant. All the publicity over a near fatality and a chute failure hadn't helped his business. Generally, everyone came out of it OK, almost like it never happened.

He wondered what he expected—a pair of shifty eyes, a cold look under a peaked cap, someone running up to exclaim he made a mistake, was sorry, and begged his forgiveness. *Sorry for what? It just happened, Bill. That's all.*

He moped around the house. Summer was almost over, and he was white from a year spent in therapy rooms. He took up lying on the chaise all day on the deck in the backyard.

Two weeks into his chaise time, on one of Mother's trips back and forth with the rose duster, she patted his head and said, "If you want a tan, why not go down to Florida, Young Man? You'd be showing appreciation to your father for everything he did over the past year and a half, not that he considers it your debt, God knows. Your leap into Ripley's wasn't free, you know. Your father could use some help with those citrus groves. Just a thought. That's all."

Bill didn't move a muscle.

"I must say, since you're trying to wear out the bottom of that chaise, I can only assume you're open to suggestions to putting some direction in your life."

He couldn't fault her on any of it. "It's kind of hot down there now, isn't it?"

"It's over ninety where you're laying, William."

Mother never had *just a thought* about anything. She always remained innocent of her off-hand remarks.

When his dad, Dick Burton, got home, Bill asked him.

"That's exactly what I want to know. What's going on in Florida?" He always made a drink before dinner during cocktail hour, so he thought that was a good time to approach him.

"I can't get down there," he continued. "Nobody calls. I call, and what do I get? The damned cracker boy saying, 'Fine. Fine. Fine. Ev-thin' jus' fine, Mista Dick.'"

"Mister Dick?" Bill snickered.

"Oh, no. No, no, no. It's Mista Dick. They're all that way. 'Now I be calling you if there's the first deal y'all gots to handle, Mista Dick.' Mista Dick my..."

"You've got that down pat, Dad. Sounds like you'd fit right in. Also sounds like pure bigotry, doesn't it?"

He tipped his head back and swallowed. Smiling, he said softly, "Uh-huh. I know. Their way of speaking isn't what I'm talking about, Son. I'm talking con job. Call it the cracker con if you want. It doesn't have a name. It's all about money, with them getting yours. It's all in code, and the code's the way they talk. If you understand the cracker dialect, you break the code. Crazy, right? Certifiable?"

Bill was taken aback. He never heard him talk that way before. "I wouldn't serve you in my bar, Dad."

"Listen, it starts out as Mista Burton, then it becomes Mista Dick when they decide you've made them your confidant. They never accept you. They tell you when you have to accept them, and there's no delay allowed. They know they're worthy, because they were born on that land. You're guilty and damn well better know it. You're a Yankee trespasser, a carpetbagger."

He took a quick swig to avoid interrupting himself and nimbly wiped his mouth with the back of the same hand. "Next, you move to being Mista Boss, within which you must now understand that they run the place, not you. The name—undoubtedly behind your back, of course—becomes still another goddamn nickname.

"They've all got their own nicknames. We know number one is Bubba. It's Bubba this and Bubba that, Little Bubba and Big Bubba, not to mention anything with Lee, Lenny Lee, Bobby Lee, Jackie Lee, and Casey Lee. That last is the name of our new grove manager down there, by the way. He's a kid named Casey Lee Christy, the one who calls me Mista Dick.

"They got their own goddamn language, and they goddamn hate us. These boys aren't from Palm Beach, you know. These are the real McCoys, the native sons, the true Floridians. It's hilarious, the craziest crap you'll ever put up with, and it's frightening, Billy."

Bill stared, his mouth agape. He tried to lick away the dryness, then gave up and just closed his mouth. There wasn't anything to say. Dad looked at him, his anger rising. Outside, he seemed reasonably calm, with his easy confidence and tiny grin, as if offering a dare or a challenge to prove him wrong. It was possible he didn't even know it was a dare.

He shoved his empty glass across the bar, and Bill silently made him a second drink and handed it over. With a frog in his throat, Dick added, "That's how it is in Florida, Son," and left the room.

Well, I asked, Bill thought, pouring a Dewar's over the rocks for himself, as he stood in the kitchen and stared out the window.

Mom was right. The chaise was looking pretty bagged out.

★   ★   ★

The Delta jet from New York touched down and rumbled along the runway through the shimmering tropical heat of West Palm Beach. It finally stopped beside the accordion mouth of the jetway.

Bill stepped through the aircraft's forward exit, and a blast of Florida's humid heat sliced across him like a torch, promptly replaced by damp, cold, air-conditioning, as he walked up the arrival concourse into a crowd from other gates.

The coats and ties and attaché cases mixed with people wearing casual resort clothes was amazing. When he remembered being there years earlier, it was quiet little Palm Beach, the winter den of the Darien Brahmins.

Things had changed, and those Brahmins weren't speaking just Ingles. Bill saw well-dressed Blacks, real-looking cowboys, and groups of Hispanics, all in every imaginable form of garb. He felt embarrassed trudging along in an old blue button-down shirt, khaki Bermudas, white legs, and old Topsiders with a wedge flip-flopping inside one heel, sunglasses bouncing on his chest. He avoided most of the crowd moving toward Baggage Claim and headed for the sign that read *Ground Transportation* carrying his canvas sailor's hanging bag and faded duffel.

He planned to get a rent-a-car and head for the beach later that evening, maybe visit the famous Ta-boo, the *"in"* restaurant. The next day he could head north for the office of Burton Groves, if there was an office. Maybe it was just a pay phone nailed to a palm tree, or a cracker boy nailed to a phone. He wasn't sure.

As he plodded down the concourse, his eyes flicked casually across faces. A guy stood off to one side up ahead, tall and tan, with combed-back white-blond hair with a hatband crease on his forehead. He was a rugged-looking thirty-five-year-old, maybe a bit older.

He certainly didn't match Dad's description of a deadbeat cracker cowboy. He wore white, stone-washed, perfect-fit Levi's and a crisp, Western-cut white shirt. One shiny-toed expensive Western boot was hiked against the wall, which was what originally caught his eye. He held a light-tan Stetson in one hand, as he scanned the crowd.

"Mista Burton!" he said sharply.

Bill flinched and stopped, then turned and looked into the man's sky-blue eyes. Putting the Stetson on his head, he extended his hand.

"Tray Robertson," he drawled. "Thought I'd do your daddy a favor. I'm at your service."

"Bill Burton, Mr. Robertson."

"Tray."

"Tray. Well, I certainly appreciate your meeting me. You work for Burton Groves?"

"No." He smiled. "I'm just a friend, a consultant so to speak. I helped your daddy in the acquisition of his fine groves up in Indian River County. I used to dabble in grove real estate. Come on. Your car's right out front."

"Tray, listen. I don't want to put you to any trouble. I was just gonna grab a rental and..."

"It's all taken care of. C'mon, Bull."

"It's Bill."

"Ah. Gotcha."

Bill thought this Tray again tried to pronounce his name when they walked under the *Ground Transportation* sign and out through the automatic doors, but he couldn't tell over the hissing hydraulics if the guy got it right. Maybe he had a mouthful of marbles. Dad said native Floridians swallowed their words.

Such thoughts evaporated when the air hit him with a wallop that took his breath away. Beyond the curb, cars reflected the heat in patterns that rippled and wavered on an asphalt grill.

Tray pointed to the curbside twenty feet from the doors. "This is yours right here."

A young, rangy Black boy popped from the driver's seat of a shimmering white Cadillac as the front doors opened, and the rear trunk lid popped up simultaneously. The boy gathered the luggage, flipped it flat in the trunk, and closed the lid.

Bill, climbing into the passenger side, felt instant relief from the air-conditioning. He watched Tray give a crisp salute to the Palm Beach County Sheriff's Deputy standing under a *NO PARKING* sign beside their car. The deputy returned the salute.

At the open driver's door, Tray slapped the boy's hand and invisibly spread a wad of green all in one smooth move. "That's an attaboy for you, Mr. Winston T. Awbrey. Yes, Sir. You get back to those Islands and say howdy to the folks, you hear? Tell your ol' Papa Roosevelt I got some news. Don't forget now."

The boy saluted like the Deputy had. Without any trace of accent, he said, "Yes, Sir, Captain Robertson. I certainly will. Thank you, Sir."

As they pulled away, Bill watched the youngster hold his salute until the Caddy went around the curve and past the covered parking toward the exit.

"Captain Robertson?" he asked with a curious smile.

Tray flicked his Stetson onto the back seat and wiped his brow. "That's my crew." He nodded. "Little Winny, a nice Bahamian boy. Some say his daddy about owns the place nowadays."

"What do you say?"

Tray's eyes were glued to the road twenty car lengths ahead through the heavy traffic. "Roosevelt T. Awbrey? At sixteen, he'd free dive seventy-odd feet straight down on Matanilla Reef and bring up eight to ten bugs at once. He had bugs stuffed in his shorts, one in his mouth and the rest in his hands. Still can. Biggest barrel chest I ever saw on a man."

"Bugs? As in Bahamian crayfish, lobster?"

"Or snapper, grouper, shark...whatever." He jigged the Cadillac into the right lane when an open space in traffic appeared.

"Do much of that?"

"Bahamas? Uh-huh. Oh, yeah."

"That's what I'd like to do."

"Bouncing around in a boat and all? Believe it, Boy. That ol' Gulf Stream's a killer, and the Bahama Bank can be a lonely desert. Lots of water out there, Okeechobee."

"As in Lake Okeechobee?"

"Yep. Seminole Indian word that means plenty big water. A Seminole Chieftain back then never lied. Our original landlords, you recall."

"Think they should have evicted us?"

"They did. We promised to be good. We lied."

Bill looked out the side window at the urban nothingness along northbound Australian Boulevard. "Looks like Florida's growing, Tray."

"Land mass is actually shrinking."

There was no question Captain-cowboy-citrus man Tray Robertson was something else.

The car was parked in front of the building, beside a sign prohibiting it, a cop guarding it for him, as if Tray owned the whole airport. Obviously knew all about the Bahamas, cruising, and boating. Then there was the name, Captain Robertson. Was he a friend of father's?

Dad's probably on the nineteenth tee at the club, hobnobbing with the heavies. This man doesn't seem like Dad's type, though there's no complaining about the Southern hospitality. Come on, Dad. This guy's hardly a con man.

Tray, easing into the right lane, turned onto Okeechobee Boulevard. "Decision time. You want to head north to where the tropics begin and citrus is king, or go straight to Palm Beach with the rest of the Yankees?"

Bill caught the jibe about Yankees. Dad said crackers hated Yankees, but he was talking about lowlifes. Tray probably just wanted to get home and rid of his passenger.

Tray inched the Cadillac into the east-turn lane, eyeing the side-view mirror. The traffic signal was red. His finger reached for the turn signal. "What's it gonna be, Boy, bores or whores?"

Bill chuckled at the choices. "You're the captain."

The light turned green, and his grin evaporated. The caddy clicked over Royal Palm Bridge to Palm Beach, the sun low behind them and a big, gleaming Hatteras sport fishing yacht, looking very much in the Palm Beach tradition, waiting to pass.

CHAPTER TWO
SKYDIVE, INC., FAIRFIELD COUNTY, CONNECTICUT AIRPORT

It all began for her on June 5, fourteen months earlier. One final time, Mickey Morgan-Lloyd checked her normally gorgeous face in the rearview mirror of the unmarked car. She was in her Plain-Jane getup, though she'd never been very plain with her unblemished ivory skin, black Sassoon coiffure tucked beneath her chin, and sea-green eyes with lashes like jet-black surf. Her face was devoid of makeup.

She was in her current cover, topped with a lucky pink baseball cap under the hood of the gray sweatshirt shielding her face. It was the opposite of her best cover, the $500-a-night look. Just below the round collar of her sweat and on the underside of her cap's peak was stenciled *MML*, her initials. Those were also her radio/telephone code name, pronounced "Emely," in case she needed backup.

Her eyes dropped and shifted a little right so she could look out the windshield and watch the miserable Southern bastard from her car—Tray Robertson. He stood in a small crowd near the right end of the line, all of them looking up, less than 100 feet away.

Interjecting her personal opinion that he was a genuine bastard was hardly professional, but she had to admit he was handsome, even so far out of his element. He didn't need Marlboro country to look like the Marlboro man—tall, tanned, a full head of white-blond hair, and handsome. That was all he had, though, just the looks. There was nothing on the inside.

She raised her field glasses for a close-up. He was clearly suffering in the temperate climate. After a week, the skin on his forehead was chalky and flaking due to lack of humidity. She noted in passing the local weather report, pertinent to parachutists, which was push-pinned to the outside bulletin board at Skydive, Inc.

> Clear, 15 mile visibility, ceiling unlimited
> Temperature 51 degrees
> Wind WNW at 10-12 knots
> Barometric pressure 30.2, steady
> Dewpoint 17
> Humidity 28%

She followed him for over a week after learning his itinerary. She knew his flight time out of Florida, arrival time in New York, the rental car he picked up to drive to Darien, Connecticut, the following morning, and when he signed up for skydiving lessons. They were at Fairfield County Airport near Darien. Tray hadn't wasted any time on his mission, whatever it was.

There was nothing official on the man's records. He'd simply been spotted among the wrong kind of "friends" in the Bahamas, specifically holding forth at the bar at the Conch Inn, Marsh Harbour, Great Abaco Island.

He looked cold out there, though he was the only one in a brown-leather, hip-length coat. Florida's cattlemen, dressed like cowboys, got more cattle than Texas.

She knew she'd have to get closer to him and would more than likely be dating him before it was over. If she got him to the edge of orgasm, he might spill something more than, "I love you whatever your name is." She would wear the necessary uniform if she must. Instead of a ponytail, pink baseball cap, and hooded sweat with the hood up, she could try a strapless black sheath and black high heels, her $500-a-night outfit.

The best bet was to watch him from the car with her binoculars. She'd parked on the grass near Skydive Inc.'s little metal building. She wasn't worried about being recognized. He'd never seen her, but it was the timing. There will be a next time.

The small crowd of 40-50 people stood on the edge of the drop zone, about a block east of the westernmost airport taxiway. The spectators looked to be mostly students in skydiving classes, prospects trying to get their nerve up, employees and curiosity seekers. Tray, along with everyone else, looked skyward.

A Cessna 182, a speck at 10,000 feet, circled, working its way windward, away from the airport traffic and the asphalt runways.

"There!" someone shouted.

The skydiver looked like a pinprick as he separated from the aircraft, which looked like a tiny black gull with its wings spread. He'd obviously cleared and arched out, maneuvering himself into the demonstration position, the free-fall mode to show to the students.

The black speck continued falling, moving slightly closer to her car. The wind was stronger aloft. He would look like a gnat on its back soon. The crowd "oohed" and "aahed."

She had him with her naked eyes, as he pulled the cord. *Show me your colors, Sky King,* she thought.

The canopy tried to mushroom.

"Open Sesame," she whispered aloud.

The crowd inhaled in unison, but it was a reverse moan. It was a streamer. The orange-and-white nylon writhed like flames.

He plunged. No reserve showed.

As the man's downward plunge suddenly ceased, her head jerked back and hit the seat rest behind her. "Jesus, God."

Her eyes on the clump embedded in the asphalt shot back to the crowd to find Tray. Her gaze went up and down the line, started over, but he wasn't there.

The miserable bastard's gone, she thought.

That wouldn't end it, though. What had been the beginning.

CHAPTER THREE
THE PALMS, INDIAN RIVER COUNTY, FLORIDA

She looked out of place, pure Rodeo Drive in hot-pink jacket and slim-cut pants accented by a deep, plunging white silk blouse and white boots. Her fawn hair was pulled back tautly with a white scarf, her complexion tawny. Midwestern chic, Eastern cool in a California body, she sat in the Palms, the dip-spittingest, shit-kickingest redneck saloon in Indian River County, Florida.

Mary Beth Holly, young schoolmarm, had been curious, brought out by his persistence. She had a date with the biggest deal in town and agreed to meet him here.

She'd checked. In the thirties, the Palms was called the Rose Garden Tea Room, *the* spot to be seen by the most-distinguished and discriminating of local high society. They waited for Henry Flagler's trains to arrive across the street.

Mary Beth observed, going in, that one of the main owners of the Palms recently added a spiral staircase to the side of the bar leading up to rooms. He also painted the exterior barn red. Things had gone downhill from there. The long bar stretched across the back of the single large room, while along the side walls were the jukebox, pinball machines, and shuffleboard. In the middle, long, rickety tables stood where brawling, cold-cocked boys actually slid along like in Western movies. Near the front door were three small tables where a fella could *set* his lady on a Saturday night. Mary Beth occupied the one closest to the exit.

The present owner did one classy thing, adding match boxes. They weren't books with paper matches but actual boxes with the words *The*

Palms above and the address below. Inside were real wooden matches a man could slip between his teeth.

The bar was on U.S. Highway 1 north of Vero Beach, a small town in Indian River County, right on the edge of an unincorporated community called Gifford, otherwise known as Niggertown, and not just by the Palms' clientele. Though a toothy, enforceable Civil Rights Act became Federal law in 1967, in Cracker County, Florida, traditional Southern mores persisted. As handy as the place might be for the local Gifford residents, no Black man dared set foot in the Palms. Closer to the truth was the fact that no Gifford resident cared to.

Mary Beth considered that admirable. She arrived early, her first mistake, and was forced to wait and watch the goings-on. No one bothered her or even tried, though she felt their eyes.

The time of her arrival was unfortunate. It was four o'clock, when the boys in cowboy boots and Levi's so low their white butts showed got off work. She knew brown bottles would soon start flying.

Hard liquor was less than popular. When consumed it was usually a ceremonial part of a self-deprecating suicide ritual resulting from unrequited love or wrecking a truck. It was all but guaranteed to clear the gun racks from every rear window of the pickups parked out back.

Good ol' boys had been a problem for Mary Beth, particularly for her new project. She was twenty-three and wanted to live in her restored house, the so-called new project, but getting help with the renovations seemed impossible.

For almost nothing, she bought an old, dilapidated home on the Indian River Lagoon, a bona fide, circa 1900 Old Florida house with wraparound porch. She planned to restore the outside to historical authenticity and transform the interior first floor to casual, smashing contemporary. The trouble was, every barnyard carpenter who came to look at the plans took one look at Mary Beth and became a wise guy.

She placed a classified ad in the local weekly and waited for it to come out on Wednesday, but no one called.

A man called who claimed to be a part-time cabinet maker—strictly as a hobby—and said he renovated two similar homes and would be pleased to show her proof of his ability. His name was Trent Robertson of the Rolling R Ranch.

His crew tore into the house two days a week, from dawn to dusk. Mr. Robertson said she was crazy to gut the downstairs. The only thing that would be left was the staircase and kitchen enclosure.

His two sons helped the first week. The older and taller of the two, a real son, Tray Robertson, was quite handsome, except his looks mattered so much to him that he couldn't bring himself to get dirty. He spent his brief stay trying to make a date with her, then he left for some political or civic call to duty, or so said his father.

Casey Lee Christy, the stepson, was different. Whole partitions went out on his back and were dropped into the flatbed truck. He was quiet, polite, and helped poor Trent with the tear-out, slapping his hat on his thigh to get rid of plaster dust. He whistled when Trent turned a nice touch on the decorative woodwork.

In close quarters, she and Casey Lee came to feel comfortable with each other. They talked and laughed. She loved his eyes, which drilled at her like those of a big cat, except they were gray, not the transparent gold of a Florida panther. At twenty-two, he was a year younger than Mary Beth.

She thought he'd be cute, except... "You'd be downright handsome if you'd get your teeth capped, Casey Lee."

"Huh?" He turned red, but then he surprised her. Coming up nose-to-nose, he said, "The hell you say. Who? How? Where you do that?" He was a pragmatist.

She wrote it all down for him.

★　★　★

A beer keg blew dry behind the bar, and the chrome tap gasped and hissed bubbling foam. The Palms clientele, to a man, cheered and whistled their approval of another dead keg.

The sound startled Mary Beth away from her thoughts of the house renovation and how she met the Robertson clan. The jukebox wailed with Boots Randolph's saxophone and Mel Tillis' visions of the real Southern men, Hank Williams, Sr., Merle Haggard, Waylon Jennings, and Johnny Cash. Mary Beth was certain that when the night came crashing down with last call, Glen Campbell would send them all, flush-faced, wide-eyed, and better than a man dare be, to Phoenix. The Palms, it seemed, had a floor show, but without the acoustics.

With a hundred eyes on her, she felt like a white morsel in a hot-pink wrapper in a cage full of drunk gorillas.

After an hour's wait, his royal highness, the hottest ticket in town, walked in—the King of the Palms, Robin of the Rednecks, and Prince of the Rolling R Ranch—Tray Robertson. She expected the mob to genuflect.

Tray slipped a matchbox under the bad leg to steady the table. Right behind him and across from Mary Beth, a wall of a man so black he was purple, sat with them.

"This is Roosevelt Awbrey, a Bahamian," Tray said, introducing the man.

Mary Beth stared at the man.

The little cowboys jamming the Palms kept their eyes to themselves, partly because Tray was royalty around here, and partly because the big Black man looked like he could bang any two of them together like cymbals.

Belinda, as Tray referred to the sour-faced redneck waitress with straw hair piled on her head and held in place with plastic combs, set a drink in front of each of them and thumped back to the bar.

"Rosey," Tray said, "I was telling Mary Beth here about the idea of putting Casey Lee Christy down at Burton Groves as manager, and she tells me this great story about..."

"Let's drop it, shall we, Tray?" Mary Beth interrupted.

"Here Casey Lee told me he got the idea himself out of a magazine."

"Tray, you're right at home here, aren't you?"

"I can only concur, Miss Holly," Roosevelt said, adding, "I'm quite surprised, Tray, you'd bring a beautiful lady here."

The man's tone was mellow and rhythmic from the Islands, but his accent was clipped, like upper-class British. Mary Beth, floored by his speech, accepted the compliment with a vague smile.

"At any rate," the big Bahamian continued, "your idea is preposterous, Tray."

Mary Beth listened, as Tray seemed determined to get Roosevelt over some kind of reticence. Tray explained that not only was it a perfect setup, but there wasn't really any choice. If they didn't put Casey Lee on the job as Burton's manager, the owner, Mr. Dick Burton, would just demand to put a stranger in that position. He even mentioned sending his son down.

"Some feel it was a disaster, Tray," Roosevelt said, "especially your fumbling theatrics in Connecticut."

"He might just come down himself," Tray continued. "I don't think we want that, now, do we?"

It was clear that whatever they were discussing, Rosey's approval was required, and it would clearly take more effort on Tray's part. As they talked, the Bahamian seemed increasingly uncomfortable with the conversation.

Tray turned to Mary Beth while trying to get Belinda's attention, too. She had never taken her eyes off their table, particularly Tray. Belinda's facial expression was one of unconcealed distaste.

"Come on, Mary Beth," Tray said, returning to the earlier subject. "What did you say to the poor kid? Belinda, another round, please."

"Tray, can't we go?"

"Not yet," he snapped.

"I can't handle the purple thing."

"What is it?" Rosey asked.

"The Redneck Special—vodka and cranberry juice."

He grimaced. "I'll stick with Dewar's and soda, if you don't mind."

Belinda was ready for their order. "The same?"

"Mineral water," Mary Beth said.

"I hope you like Mountain Dew," Tray quipped. "Come on. How'd you handle Casey Lee?"

Mary Beth shrugged. "We were talking. I wondered if he had a girl. It just came out. I told him I'd like to be friends with him and gave him some advice."

"What advice?"

"I said, in my opinion, he'd be perfect if he got his teeth fixed."

"Got his... Did he?"

"Oh, he got 'em capped. He's beautiful."

"I haven't seen that."

"You could try seeing him at your dad's place," she said sarcastically. "The Rolling R, where your mail goes? You ought to drop by sometime."

She watched the Black man becoming impatient. He wasn't apparently the type to sit around and kibitz.

Whatever Roosevelt wanted to discuss, it had to do with giving young Casey Lee a job at what he called "a damned important place like Burton's." He wasn't about to get into that in front of Mary Beth, though.

He quietly lacerated Tray a couple times, saying he was too damned casual and careless, and Mr. Hector Caraja wouldn't tolerate it. He glanced around the room after he mentioned the Columbian name, then glared at Tray.

Tray rolled over his comment, saying it was better and safer if they put their own man in there.

Rosey chuckled without humor. "Casey Lee is hardly our own man. Besides, he's just a kid."

"He's twenty-two and never has to know anything. He'll just do as he's told. I can handle my little stepbrother like usual."

Finally, Rosey said, "I really must leave, Tray. Miss Holly, a pleasure." He stood, and the whole front door and wall disappeared behind his broad back. "Come see us in paradise."

"Thank you, Rosey. Where, exactly, is home?"

"The Bahamas, Miss Holly. Tray, take care. I'll be aboard the yacht for a few days then back at my place. Talk to me." It wasn't an invitation.

The barrel-chested man, ducking low through the doorway, walked onto the street.

Belinda stood at their table with two Dewar's and a Mountain Dew.

"Thank you, Belinda, Darlin'," Tray said. "I'll take his and the check, please."

"Well, you got it." She circled the table. "Anything you say, Big Cowman."

She set a glass of sickly sweet fizzle in front of the lady, no ice, and added a straw.

"Thank you," Mary Beth said, looking up.

Belinda's face was set in stone. What was odd, her expression didn't improve when she glanced at Tray.

After the waitress was gone, Mary Beth asked, "Who is Roosevelt Awbrey, and what's your connection with him?"

Tray sipped his drink, and it almost went down the wrong pipe. He brushed off his shirt front. "Roosevelt T. Awbrey is the best dive and fishing guide in the Islands, or he was. He's a big man nowadays, though he's only twenty-four. He built up the economies of a number of islands by putting people to work."

"He developed resorts and hotels?"

"Yeah, and jobs and schools and hospitals."

"On the six figures he makes a year as a dive guide?"

"With help, I'm sure, from the British Crown Governor. The Bahamians probably have economic development programs, along with private donations and friends."

"Of course." Trying to hold eye contact, she gave him a tiny smirk. "Friends and all. Quite complicated, I'm sure."

He tried to keep looking at her but couldn't, so he looked down and brushed his shirt. "I don't know much about it, Mary Beth, not yet."

*   *   *

Roosevelt Awbrey's best client came along after he reached his teens. It was short, fat Mr. No Wet, the Columbian from Miami, Hector Caraja, who liked to throw money around.

By then, Rosey was a master dive guide out of Walkers Cay in the northern Bahamas and had a strong body, expanded chest, and powerful arms and legs from diving. He wasn't finished growing yet, either.

Hector liked to sit in the fishing cockpit in a portable fighting chair all day, one hand on the fishing rod and the other on his glass. Not counting his early hits, he drank rum Collins, rum and orange juice, or rum and Coke constantly, except when he waved and cheered Rosey for the trophies the boy brought up—hog snapper, strawberry grouper, or lobster. His girlfriend sunbathed, at least until Rosey climbed back aboard. Then she went to work.

Sometimes, she got lucky when her Uncle Hector drank too much. By late afternoon, Mr. No Wet lurched into the main cabin with its air-conditioning and stumbled to his stateroom for a nap.

She pulled out all the stops then, though Rosey did his best to put her off. If reported, fucking the clients was the only good way a guide could lose his job. She was unabashed, though, and very hungry with her lean, delicious body in her tiny bikini.

Inevitably, she overcame Rosey's insistence and brought him down in broad daylight on the aft fishing deck.

On the last day of Mr. No Wet's stay at Walkers Cay Club, he still hadn't inserted a single toe into the beautiful Bahamian waters. He lay by the pool "up the hill," as people referred to the hotel built on the crest of a hill fifty feet above sea level, the only significant elevation in that part of the island chain.

His feet dangling in the mechanically desalinated water, a rum and Coke in his hand, Mr. No Wet looked over the endless, shimmering spectrum of blue and green of the Bahamas Bank that mesmerized every eye that gazed upon it, and thought.

Rosey decided that *thinking* was Mr. No Wet's longest suit. When Rosey received an order from the front desk, he immediately went to the pool. Mr. No Wet rolled over and up, threw a terrycloth jacket over his shoulders, and gestured toward a cabana table.

At first, the boy listened casually, being polite to yet another white client who was slightly goofy from too much sun, booze, and money. The natives called it "island fever." The fat little man seemed to be thinking out loud to himself, anyway.

Then Rosey sensed the man was, indeed, talking directly to him, and he was very serious, making offers, suggestions, and guarantees. What he offered could change Rosey's life forever.

Rosey would go to school in Europe all expenses paid. First he would attend an English prep school, then university. During holidays, he would be placed at the French Bourse, the London Exchange, a Bay Street Bank, and then a large international bank in Miami, followed by an equally prestigious investment banking firm. He would become an articulate gentleman, an expert in currency exchange, credit, international money transfers, and financial matters in general.

"When you're ready," the man said, "I put you to work for me."

"Where about I be when I work for you, Mon?" Rosey, of course, was skeptical. The little fat man had treated him fairly so far. Maybe he would send Rosey to Nassau for some reason.

"After education, you come right back here and live. That's what I want you to do. Live here, be a dive guide in your spare time. I give you assignments, you do them, and you come back here to home."

"Why you do this for me?"

The little fat man leaned forward to look into Rosey's eyes. Taking a white envelope from his pocket, he flipped it across the table. "Today, you'll teach me to catch a lobster, right on the bottom, the whole deal. Tomorrow when we leave, you get started on school.

"There's ten grand in that envelope. We'll buy you a new business suit, whatever you like. Go to the boutique in the club right fuckin' now and get yourself a flashy new bathing suit, one with a jock in it. Every time you bend over for two fuckin' weeks, your whole goddamn program's been dangling in my face. You upset the girlfriend, the fuckin' whore. Put it on my account."

Frowning at the man's language, Rosey started to rise, but the man put his hand over Rosey's which was on the envelope.

"What do you think, Kid? Yes or no."

Rosey hesitated. "No. I don't think even Rosey teach you to catch the lobster." He would tell Momma, *Man from Miami, he likes me, send me to school somewhere. Wants me to work for him.*

She would be astonished and start praying.

Then Rosey grinned. "Yes, I work for you, and I get gentleman's accent for you, Mr. Care-a-jaw." He couldn't pronounce the name correctly.

"Hector," the fat little Columbian said, smiling. "Call me Hector."

"Roosevelt."

*   *   *

As an adult, Rosey was a brute of a man, yet innocent and shy-faced, jovial, inquisitive, and soft-voiced, with both a lilt and a clip. He was still the finest diver in the Islands.

He hung in the deep water, nearly neutral in buoyancy like a giant jewfish, and used his finger and thumb to hold onto a cave that cut into the coral head. He swayed in the wispy current that brought cooler, cold, then warm temperatures continuously over him. Despite his bulk, he was able to blend into his environment, surrounded by groupers, black and yellow angelfish, purple hogfish, and schools of yellowtail. Young barracudas, with insatiable curiosity, prodded and poked his face and neck, always staring.

High above, a bullet-shaped Hatteras hull bobbed on a tin foil surface. Columns of speckled light undulated in descending shards, halting only at the top of the formation, leaving the face and cave mouth dark in shadow. Enough twig-like antennae flicked and tickled at the cave's upper brow to show they were there in the hundreds. *Panulirus Argus,* as a London textbook called them. To Rosey, as a Bahamian, they were bugs—lobster.

He tickled back at the antennae, waving the tips of his gloved hand, extending it down, so they could sense movement. The antennae extended, trying to learn more.

Suddenly, he rolled smoothly down over the brow in a slow-motion somersault. With a scissor stroke of his legs, he was face-up under the cap and inside the cave.

He picked off two, popped them into his bright yellow bathing suit, grabbed two more, holding onto one and biting the hard carapace of the other with his teeth, then snatched a runaway and held it.

The attack was over as quickly as it began without even clouding the water. A nurse shark remained slumbering at the back of the cave.

Looking up toward the surface, he began his much-needed ascent. He saw the White man with the white-blond hair through the grate of the teak dive platform hanging off the Hatteras' transom.

The new client was a young rancher or citrus man or both, age about thirty, from Florida. He handled the big boat like a pro, like all the citrus guys could. He leaned over the water, staring down with his eyes shaded by one hand.

Rosey needed air, but he still had a little time. He bit harder on his mouthful, so close to the surface he wanted to blow and inhale, but the most-famous free diver in the Bahamas always came up with one in his mouth. He kicked hard, rising like a great, brown-skinned Blue Marlin, ready to burst forth and dance on the water. He couldn't wait any longer.

The last cubic inches of air exploded from him, as he broke the surface, erupting it into froth. He rose almost free of the foam, as if to shake the bait and spat his mouthful into the flailing arms of the surprised White man who barely managed to swat the thing into the boat.

"Jesus Christ, Roosevelt!" the shocked client said.

Rosey, thrashing in the foamy water, held up his trophies as if they were made of gold. "I say, Old Boy! Mr. Tray, come in quick. If it isn't a veritable condominium of lobster down there, I swear your name isn't Tray Robertson, Mon."

*　*　*

Evening arrived at the Palms. The good ol' boys had mostly gone home. Dinner would be on the table before sundown across Cracker County, regardless.

Tray never answered Mary Beth's question about who and what Roosevelt Awbrey was. She kept her eyes on him, seeing him thinking hard.

Finally, something meshed for him, and he looked up, pleased. "Come on. I'm taking you to a gorgeous new place, the new yacht club called Riomar Bay. It's lobster night. We can't be late."

Mary Beth looked at him a long time, then said, "I'm sorry, Tray. Take me home."

It was too strange. She hadn't understood a single thing in the conversation between Tray and the Bahamian. She couldn't believe that she, of all people, couldn't understand spoken English. Though she knew each word, they didn't have the right meaning. She felt sad and a little sick.

Trent Robertson suggested he'd like to see her go out with young Tray and get to know him better. She wondered if Trent knew of Tray's giant Bahamian friend with the tinge of a British accent and the Columbian friend.

She'd call him and explain, saying she'd started feeling sick at the Palms and asked to go home. Because she and Trent were friends, she could ask him about the odd conversation.

CHAPTER FOUR
PALM BEACH, LIFE IN THE GRAND MANNER

"I'm at the Breakers." Mickey knew the celebrated impact of that sentence was all in how it's said—delivery controlled effect. She had to purr the words, yet toss them out like a castoff over her shoulder, preferably a luscious, naked shoulder, while the words remained clear. She floated the line like a tiny tidal wave across the rooms of expensive restaurants.

Heads turned. Mouths gaped. Crystal froze, and tinkling sterling silver stopped moving.

For nearly a century on Palm Beach, those words exceeded the mere sentence. They were a statement meaning, *Life in the grand manner is still for sale, right here, right now, and I'm buying.*

"I'm at the Breakers," she cooed to Jimmy, the cabbie, at three A.M. in front of the Taboo Restaurant on Worth Avenue.

"You got it, Mick, Baby."

She never had to wait.

Born "on the island," as the old guard referred to Palm Beach, Mickey moved on, but Mother and Daddy Morgan-Lloyd still lived there on their ocean spread and in an uneasy retirement.

Their problem wasn't money—far from it—or health. It was shock at their daughter's chosen profession.

"Go ahead and turn on the meter this time, Jimmy."

"What? And take the chance of losing you?"

The cab made a U-turn. A few hundred yards later, it swung north onto County Road. In a mile, they turned east for the ocean.

The cab passed landscaping so valuable and rare, tours of it were conducted daily to show off the putting and bowling greens and the bent grass lawns.

On final approach, Mickey always expected trumpets heralding royalty and the ooga-ooga of Roaring '20's Roadsters jammed with shrieking flappers. Then there it was, the misty, floodlit twin belvedere towers against the hot Atlantic night, the living monument to life in the grand manner, the Breakers Hotel.

They circled the Grand Entry with its fifty-foot Florentine fountain at the center and stopped near the towering entrance. Mickey stuck a black high heel and long, dark, sheer-hosed leg out the open cab door, and a crisp, observant doorman assisted her. His expression showed she was an out-and-out dream.

Mickey was in her early twenties, with a lightly tanned complexion and a black, natural Sassoon hairdo that curled under her chin and around her leaf-green eyes, surrounding full but professionally perfect makeup. She wore a stunning, strapless black sheath, and her time was purportedly worth $500 a night, off season.

She casually pointed a long, slim finger back at the cab.

"And this would be...?" the doorman asked, leaning stiffly into the taxi and flexing his nose.

"The name's Bill Burton."

"How splendid."

"Tray Robertson already here?"

"Yes, indeed." The doorman was apparently repelled by the memory and rolled his eyes. "Mr. Robertson has...retired."

The doorman waved a young bellboy over to help. The boy spotted Mickey and nearly froze in midstep. She did that to some.

The doorman placed one of Bill's limp arms over his shoulder and behind his neck. The bellboy mimicked him on the other side, and they escorted the sleepy traveler up the broad stone steps, his shiny shoe tips scuffing and bopping through the front door into one of the most-magnificent examples of Florentine art in the world—the main lobby. Priceless pieces of furniture stood like guards. Massive 15th century tapestries hung on the walls, and the frescoed ceilings were stunning.

Mr. Burton, at a perfect angle to observe, had his eyes closed.

A concierge slipped the bellboy a key, Mickey followed the luggage, Burton's raggedy canvas bags and her huge tote.

Around 8:00 A.M., Bill heard Mickey up and moving around. He lay on his stomach on a soft Breakers' hotel king double, his face to the side on a sweaty pillow with a pounding head and dry mouth. Hearing the lightly fluttering, filmy drapes, he felt the gentle ocean breeze on his back with a warm morning sun.

She placed a towel filled with ice under his head. Through half-closed eyes, he saw her standing over him, rubbing baby oil into her hands. She looked fabulous with her slim legs, hair, perfect makeup, and a pair of 36s that stood out unassisted. Taken as a whole, she called the ensemble "the uniform." Kneeling beside him, she rubbed him down with the oil.

When she finally rolled him onto his back, his erection stood up proudly, proving, among other things, that his night on the Palm Beach Strip hadn't been fatal. She covered him with the sheet.

Mickey brought over the tray left by room service holding two double vodka, double fire, Bloody Marys each.

After sipping, Bill said, "Jesus, God, that's good. I just died and went to heaven."

She knocked back her Bloody Mary in two long gulps and refilled her glass. "No, we don't get to heaven until ten. We've got an hour's flight time left. Any suggestions for starting off your first official day as a Floridian?"

He moaned.

"I've got an idea."

They played Mickey's unique brand of sex Charades for most of the hour, and she let him win every time. Finally, she climbed down off the rail of the outside balcony overlooking the ocean, went inside, and walked toward the bathroom. No one down on the beach bothered to look up. If they had, they wouldn't have believed what was taking place high over the white sands of the Breakers. At least that suggested they weren't being watched from the surrounding grounds.

"Ten o'clock," she announced. "Robertson wants you to meet him by the pool. You'd better shower. Come on, Silly."

They were running a little late.

When Bill emerged from the bathroom all clean-shaven and smartly dressed, he looked very splendid, indeed.

"Wow," Mickey said. "You'd better go ahead on down."

"Are you always so gorgeous?" Bill asked at the door.

They pecked like married folks, then he walked toward the elevator.

Alone, Mickey, squeaky clean and devoid of makeup, her hair in a ponytail, slipped into a fresh white bra and panties, white sport shirt, white shorts, her warm-up jacket, anklets, and tennis shoes. She plopped dark aviators over her eyes and put on a pink baseball cap, pulling her hair through the back strap.

Taking a new Head tennis racket from her jock bag, she carefully folded her black dress and placed it, along with the black heels, makeup kit, and other duds, into the bag and zipped it shut. Racket in hand and bag over her shoulder, she walked out the door.

Her usual method in such places was to take the least-visible route. In this case, it was the south doors, out under the green-and-white striped awnings that connected the hotel with the beach club and into old reliable from Ace Beach Taxi of the Palm Beaches.

The taxi waited with the passenger door open. She tossed in her bag ahead of her, slipped into the back seat, and held her racket. Looking through the strings, she pressed them against her forehead until they left marks, while the taxi passed the big fountain held up by the naked Grecian figures.

Mickey surmised that her overnight roommate was pretty straight, which was fine with her. She liked him, which helped.

It was the way she played the role. If she didn't like a guy, she'd just as soon kick him in the balls and hightail it. Her current so-called clientele could run pretty rough, but fear of retribution was minimal. No hood wanted his friends to know a hooker walked out on him.

She hated the bad guys—particularly the stinking drug dealers and opioid traffickers with their flowery Cuban shirt collars outside their loud sport coats, their planes, boats, guns. They smelled dirty, talked dirty, and were fouling life in Florida.

Mickey was dedicated. *That guy Burton could be a good little citrus king if he's clean and stays that way,* she thought. *Also if he stays away from that other shit. He seems smart.*

She listened to him before Robertson got him drunk the previous night, and he had some pretty damn good ideas.

Later, he became very funny, though she had to pay attention to catch his dry, subtle, and cutting humor. He had lots of hospital jokes. His monologue on the accident was hysterical. Maybe it shouldn't have been, but it was, or at least she thought so. Tray never seemed to laugh at anything, even when Burton attempted a soft-shoe number on the Taboo's bar top.

She also knew in South Florida, a person could end up with broken legs or worse if he didn't mind his own business. Mickey knew her job and was very good at it.

When she caught herself wondering if there was the slightest chance he might call her, she asked herself, *Lady, who are you shitting?*

"You say something, Mickey?" the cabbie asked.

"Yeah, Jimmy. I said 'Worth Avenue, please.'" Shopping usually helped her thinking. Somehow, she had to get back on track.

★   ★   ★

As Bill approached, he saw Robertson slouched at the Breakers' Tiki Hut Bar overlooking the sparkling hotel pool, tended by a Filipino in a white waistcoat.

Rows of lounges and cabana tables with green-and-white umbrellas, mostly occupied by women, encircled the pool. Robertson wore his Levi's and Stetson.

All the ladies around the pool, from the older, slim, face-lifted, leathery blondes to the young, slim, lithe, bronze blondes, appeared to be auditioning for Frontier Woman of the Year, but Tray ignored them.

Bill snaked his way through the bikinis.

Tray held out a little black shoe wedge. "The Taboo Restaurant sent it over. They said they didn't need it. They already have your heel marks all over the bar to remember you by." He swallowed the remainder of a cool cranberry and vodka and asked. "You ready to move?"

"Oh, jeez. Thanks." Bill slipped the wedge into his shoe and signaled the bartender. "I just want to say good-bye to Mickey. Bloody Mary, please," he told the bartender.

"She's gone."

"She said she'd be right down."

"You hear a meter running?"

"No. Why?"

"She's gone, Boy."

Bill chuckled but didn't mean it. When his Bloody Mary arrived, he took a swig, glanced at Tray and chuckled again. Somehow, he was cast as the dumb yokel, and Robertson was Mr. First Nighter. *Shouldn't that be the other way around?* Bill wondered.

I got myself a Class-A hangover, don't I?

Although it should have been obvious, he hadn't thought of Mickey as a prostitute even once. They kissed like they were married.

"She's quite a girl," he said.

"Best hooker on Palm Beach," Tray agreed. "That's one gorgeous bitch."

Bill studied the labels on the bottles behind the bar. "Yeah. Well, thanks for taking care of that. How much do I owe you?"

"Forget it, Friend." Tray raised his glass. "Welcome to sunny Florida." He drained it and set it on the bar. "Let's get outta here, Mr. Burton. The Burton Groves staff's expecting to meet you. They got the office fixed up and everything. You ready?"

"I guess. What staff? We have an office?"

"Sure do, an old, double-wide mobile home I used to use on the ranch as my "office." Casey Lee rented it and put it in the groves. He fixed it up professionally. He's got an office, you have one, and Penny's up front. She's Casey Lee's secretary, and now yours."

"How'd they, you, everybody know I was coming?"

"Your daddy called me, and I called them."

Something about that didn't jive, but Bill couldn't pin it down. "Sounds good. Let's cut back through the hotel on the way out." He hoped to catch Mickey. "It's cooler inside."

Tray held up a finger and nodded. "That-a-way." He pointed through the cabana tables.

An oiled squadron of broiled midriffs relaxed in unison as the two men left, and the women stopped posturing.

They walked from the Beach Club, across the awninged lane, past the vacant cab stand, and into the cool hotel. Bill marveled at the ceilings and almost tripped over a wing-backed chair, as the main lobby widened before him.

Did I walk through this last night? he wondered.

Tray headed for the front doors, while Bill turned toward the main desk and said over his shoulder, "Be right with you."

When Bill stopped and opened his mouth to speak, one of the many clerks behind the massive desk said, "Good morning, Mr. Burton. These are for you."

He handed Bill a white business envelope with the Breakers watermark attached to a scroll of white tissue paper cinched by a red ribbon.

Bill snapped open the ribbon and held up a single, long-stemmed red rose. The clerks muttered their approval, and a dozen guests gave soft applause. More than slightly confused and not a little embarrassed, Bill tore open the envelope and saw five new $100 bills and a small card with a message.

Enclosed please find deposit for skydiving lessons as promised. Please call.
  M.

When Bill walked outside, he saw Tray already in the driver's seat of the Cadillac with the trunk open. Bill set his open bag in the trunk, carefully placed the envelope inside, zipped it, and put the tissue-covered rose on top.

The doorman closed the trunk. When Bill offered a tip, the man refused, gesturing to indicate that Tray had already handled it. Bill sat in the passenger seat.

As they headed north on the Florida Turnpike, Bill looked out the window, amazed at how fast the scenery changed. Two miles north of Palm Beach, the buildings, crowds, noise, and traffic vanished. They went over the Okeechobee Waterway Bridge, where the Turnpike crested the Florida Ridge, and saw citrus groves as far as he could see.

Tray kept a heavy foot on the accelerator for over an hour, though he frequently glanced in the rearview mirror for cops. Bill and Tray didn't speak.

Tray seemed to be concentrating on the road and was deep in thought. Bill felt the man look at him in the mirror or turn his head to look directly, as if studying him.

Bill glanced back as if to say, *You're all right, and I'm all right.*

The poor guy probably just wanted to get home. Meeting the flight and offering a lift was one thing. He'd have to tell Dad, although he'd just say he'd been well cared for and not get into details about Mickey. Still, the whole thing took up twenty-four hours of Tray's time, not to mention the tab.

Holy shit! The tab!

As they passed the Ft. Pierce exit sign, Tray put on the turn signal. Bill felt he had to say something before he forgot.

"I know what you tried to do, Tray..."

He suddenly realized why Tray had been so quiet. The car squealed to a stop, blocking the toll booth ramp. Tray's door flew open, and he leaned out to vomit violently on the asphalt.

"...and I appreciate it," Bill finished, talking to the back of the man's head.

Once they were through the Turnpike tollbooth, Tray wanted to stop at a bar. He promised to show Bill how to get along and how life worked in Fort Pierce.

They stopped at one bar, then at several more. When they were finally back on the road, Bill wondered, *Are we there yet?*

Finally, after driving west on an endless dirt road, when it was well past five o'clock in the afternoon, Tray said, "We're here."

CHAPTER FIVE
BULL

Suddenly, Tray pointed through the windshield just before the dirt road curved north. "That's him."

Straight ahead, staring back at them, a figure leaned against a dust-covered pickup, one cowboy boot that matched the dusty road hiked up against the front bumper.

Two other vehicles were parked side-by-side beside the pickup in a dirt parking area bulldozed from a grapefruit grove. Beyond the parking, all but swallowed up by fruit trees, was a bleached-out beige doublewide mobile home.

Seeing the arch classic Florida Cracker his dad described, Bill thought, *That's gotta be him.*

Fifty feet away, the man came off exactly as advertised.

The car pulled into the soft, sandy parking area, stopped, and the two men got out.

From the road, the man looked like a gritty old cowpoke, but up closer, when Bill saw his face, he realized he was wrong. He was young, had dark wavy hair, was clean-shaven, and was all muscle in his cowhand duds—a redneck Marlboro Man.

Bill expected the man to step forward any second and greet them, but he didn't move.

"Evening, Casey Lee," Tray said.

When that didn't trigger a reaction, Tray whispered, "Guess we're late." He tapped Bill to step forward.

Bill tried a smile, thinking they were close to the same age. "Hi. I'm Bill Burton." He held out his hand, trying to look the guy in the eyes, which were as wild and gray as storm clouds. "You must be Casey Lee Christy."

The young man moved a wood match from one side of his mouth to the other, exposing a perfect set of white teeth. He centered the match, flipped it over, sucked on it, and didn't speak.

Without a glance at the extended hand, he spat the match to the ground, turned his back on them, and started down the path toward what had to be the office. The doublewide had a sign mounted over the door that read *Burton Groves, Inc.*

"Yep," Casey called over his shoulder. "You got that right."

Tray, a step behind Bill, said softly, "He's been waiting since yesterday."

"Casey Lee?" Bill called. "Why don't I meet you first thing in the morning?"

Casey Lee stopped with his back to them.

"Say around eight?"

He started walking again.

"That's like noon to him," Tray said.

"How about seven?"

Casey Lee stopped and turned. "By seven, we'll be done with split-fruit inspections on two groves. By eight, be half-done with cross-sections of acid-sugar ratio samplings we gotta have, 'cause crops coming in, as any man can see. Just look around you. It's been hot and wet."

He muttered something about "a dumb fucking Yankee," which Bill didn't quite hear.

"Six?"

Casey Lee started back down the path toward them. There might be the hint of a smirk or smile in the creases outside his eyes, above the slightly raised cheekbones.

When he stood in front of the pair again, he said, "Tray, don't you have someplace to be other than here?"

The last thing Tray wanted was to be caught in the middle of something. "Hell, yeah. Well, you guys don't need me, so I'm outta here. Hey, you don't have a car."

"I'll take care of him," Casey Lee said.

Tray quickly opened the caddy's trunk and draped the hanging bag over Bill's arms while pitching the duffle at Casey Lee. The long-stemmed rose fell to the ground in front of Casey Lee.

He picked it up and examined it before holding it out to Tray. "Trophy goes with you, I take it?"

"Nope. His," Tray said.

Casey Lee nodded and bit his lip, as if considering the implications, and handed the rose to Bill.

Tray slammed the trunk closed, got behind the wheel, rolled down the window, and backed out. Bill trotted alongside the window.

"Thanks for getting me at the airport," Bill said. "I really appreciate..." The car roared off.

As Tray disappeared ahead of the dust trails, Casey Lee pointed to the group of vehicles parked in front of the office.

"The four-wheel drive pickup there, that's me. The green Jeep Wagoneer can be you. Fact is, you own it. The VW is Penny's."

"Penny?"

She stood in the open office doorway, a tiny blonde and a devastating figure in her jeans, which seemed the approved dress code for the job.

"Mr. Christy calls me indispensable," Penny said, giggling, "but ya gotta consider the source, ya know? I'm Penny Turner, Sir."

Bill had to hand it to the Cracker boys. They knew how to pick more than grapefruit. "Hi, Penny. Bill Burton."

They stepped inside and dropped his hanging bag on the floor with the duffel on top and the rose on top of that.

"So nice to finally make your acquaintance, Mr. Burton, sir. That your rose?"

"How about you just call me Bill, Penny?"

She nodded. "If there's anything at all I can do for you, Sir, Bill, let me know. Dizzy as I am, I flat do it all—payables, receivables, books, letters, phones, and truck radios. I'll see y'all tomorrow, hear? It's late."

Bill looked at his watch. "Boy it is." It was after six. "Hope you weren't waiting around just for me."

"Oh, it was worth it." She moved toward the door and glanced at the rose. "I didn't really pay attention to what the rednecks around here said about you, anyway."

She turned back, nodding to the rose. "Congratulations." More loudly, she said, "Night, Casey Lee."

Casey Lee's office was at one end, with Bill's at the opposite end. The center had been gutted and refitted with self-standing office partitions separating various workstations.

Penny's desk sat in the middle, facing the door. She was obviously the receptionist, too. The whole place was panel-boarded, draped, carpeted, and clean. It even had a tiny kitchen.

This sure beats hell out of New York or Darien, Bill thought. "I like your accommodations, Casey Lee, right out here in the groves and everything. Very comfy, too. I..."

"These here are your offices." Casey Lee was trying to be cordial. "It says Burton on the front door. I'm just a hired hand, but folks flat did some work. I'm glad you like 'em."

"Did we need the expense? That's what I'm wondering."

Casey Lee stiffened again. "Depends on what you're trying to do."

"Meaning?"

"Frankly?"

"I may be misjudging you, but I don't think so," Bill said. "I think frankly is the only way you play, and I sure would prefer it that way."

There was that tiny hint of a grin again. "It depends on whether you want to just continue your daddy's little tax dodge here, or..." He waffled his hand.

"Or?"

They spoke simultaneously.

"Make something happen."

"Get it on."

"How much we got in acres?" Bill asked.

"About three thousand."

"I thought it was four."

"I been quoting that to various people, your father for one, but we're just in contract for the last thousand, actually. We're waiting for your approval."

"A thousand acres of groves? How much?"

"It's not all producing grove land. There's some thirty-year-old trees, some nutrient poor. Some people think a grove is a good grove or a bad grove. I don't care. I care about where. Average grower would call it junk. That's the whole idea. It's a steal, but it's around two million dollars."

"Jesus. What if we don't have or can't...?"

"We're out," Casey Lee drawled casually. "Out of business, period. Look. There's no sweat right now. See, we do business a little different around here. Where you come from, everything's in writing, right? All contracts are in writing, and nobody trusts anybody.

"Down here in the citrus business, nothing is in writing. In fact, if you ask for it in writing, nobody would do business with you. They'd be insulted. Worse, they'd never trust you. Down here, contracts are oral, sealed with a handshake. A man's word is his bond. It's been like this forever."

"And everybody out here is as honest as the day is long, right?" Bill asked sarcastically.

"Doesn't matter. You break a contract around here, you're out. The embargo against you is in. One hour and it's on every CB radio into every pickup within range. The following day, all those CBs have relayed, and everyone in the state knows. Nobody will risk doing business with you, because if they do, then they're out, too. Nobody will buy or sell from you. You're dead."

"How long before we're dead?"

"Well," Casey Lee leaned back in his chair, his hands behind his head. "We got a healthy down payment behind the contract, but I never bit off a thousand before. That's where you come in."

"Me?"

He leaned forward. "You may be the last to hear about this, but you're already a big name in the citrus business around here."

Bill settled in his chair to listen.

"See, well, you're probably not gonna like this, but just listen for a minute. First, we've given you a nickname. You're Bull Burton."

"Jesus! Tray's been calling me that. I thought he was saying 'Bill' with a mouthful of…"

"Marbles?" Casey Lee grinned. "Silver-tongued Tray Robertson, our next senator? He was the first one I told. I said that's what your friends call you, and he should, too. I made it emphatic. Tray's got the biggest mouth in the South.

"You're Bull all over these parts already. You're looking at me funny. Here's how this plays. It's a nickname from your hard-driving success up north. You go after things and get what you want. The word is you're a boy millionaire in your own right in addition to being the only son of one of the wealthiest families in New York City. It hasn't hurt any that you go 'round jumping out of airplanes without a parachute, either.

"Let me finish. You're a genius in market analysis, price estimating, propagation, fertilizing—all the latest in scientific, ecological stuff. You got international market connections, especially Japan. You're Bull. Best of all, you hit the USDA citrus crop estimate right on the money."

"I'm sorry. I seem to have forgotten what the fuck a U.S. whatever-it-is."

"You're the boys who announce what the crop will be, how big it is, based on your vast experience and intelligence, before the official USDA announcement from the United States Department of Agriculture. Of course, if you really know, you price accordingly. Most important, if you're close or right on, as in your case, everybody thinks you know everything. Crazy?"

"This whole thing is crazy. *You're* crazy."

"Yup, it is, and I am. I've spent my whole life watching these so-called experts and believe me, crazy or not, this will do the trick for us."

"And having achieved this esteemed reputation, what do I do?"

Casey Lee shifted back into his drawl and pretended his back ached. "Ya know, I don't go in banks 'less I have to. At least, I don't try to borrow from banks. Here's how I see it. Impressions count, as I'm sure you know. Around here, I'm still just a poor dumb Cracker boy from Blue Cypress swamp. You understand me, Mista Burton?"

Bill sat back and looked at the young man sitting across the desk. Dad's performance at the cocktail hour in the kitchen in Darien flooded back to him. *Bubba this. Bubba that. Lenny Lee and Bobby Lee and Casey Lee. Everybody's got a nickname, Bill. It's the Cracker con game.*

He didn't know whether to hug Casey Lee or run for his life.

"Now listen. Banks here make loans expressly for tax-shelter purposes so fast, with no thought to risk or profit, that these young loan officers fresh out of Yankee business schools feel like big shots. You can hear 'em telling their girlfriends every night in the local bars, bragging to everybody, including themselves.

"Banks aren't watching. They're too busy growing and competing with each other. You watch. In twenty or thirty years, a lot of these 'sure thing' mortgages will still have never seen a payoff. The pinstriped suit that isn't even shiny yet is gone, 'cause no bank could pay him $75,000 in his second year. There's no loyalty, supervision, or community concern.

"I know about citrus. Tomorrow morning, I'll show you the nicest, most flushed-out groves, the healthiest trees and best-looking fruit in Indian River District. We're fighting greening. I've got a hell of a lot more expansion ideas than just this thousand-acre deal, which, by the way, will top $25,000 an acre someday soon in my opinion. But no question about it, I've got my limitations, and..."

Good ol' Dad was half right about these Florida Crackers. They'll con not only the Yankees but their own kind, too. I was Bull Burton long before I heard the name. I want to cheer that we might actually do this by ourselves without asking the old man to do it for me. Maybe I can cut the cord in the process.

In a low-slung Southern drawl that surprised even himself, he said, "Don't sweat it, Boy. We'll kill 'em."

Casey Lee was shocked. He stood slowly, as if he'd never seen Bill before, and a big grin spread across his face. "You mean you're gonna go for it?"

"What have we got to lose, Man?" *Just everything,* echoed back.

Casey Lee grabbed Bill's hand across the desk and shook it hard, then shook it some more. "Welcome aboard Bill Burton. "Shee-it!"

"Hey, Boy, that's Bull Burton." He tried to look sloe-eyed. "Y'all can call me Bull, hear?"

"Shee-it!"

★　★　★

Bouncing along a marl road in the pitch black, clutching his morning coffee, Bill thought it was the darkest predawn morning the world ever knew. Without the washboard road and engine sounds, if he stared out the pickup's side window, he couldn't even tell they were moving. The bright-white pillars of mist the headlights sent out were hacked off by black nothingness fifty yards ahead. He wondered if the Crackers called it late or early.

Casey Lee turned the wheel, and the headlights swung through waist-high grass and stopped. The beams filled with mist and dust, while mosquitoes swarmed in and out of the light.

Over the hood, Bill saw a wooden gate blocking the trail with a sign that read *Burton Grove No. 3.*

Casey Lee and the gate disappeared, as he walked it open.

"Dark enough for you?" Bill asked, as Casey Lee reappeared out of nowhere and climbed back behind the wheel.

"Dirty old road through a citrus grove don't get any blacker." He set the four-wheel drive. "By the way, watch yourself out here. There's nobody for miles if you get hurt or bit."

Bill wiped coffee off the front of his long-sleeved shirt. Casey Lee told him earlier, "I'd suggest long sleeves on the outside chance a mosquito lands on ya."

"Bit?" he asked. "Did you mean bit with teeth?"

"Fangs. Diamondbacks. They love to cross the road early, when it's still dark. They're starting to mate about now. It happens in fall and spring, so they're on the move."

He glanced at Bill's feet. "You got boots on, right? Wrong. Going yachting, were you? We'll have to get you some good, cheap cowboy boots. Matter of fact, we'll fit you out like a first-class dude for going to the bank, too. You walk in, and them pinstriped bean counters are gonna swoon. By the way, before we get all the way out to the grove, I want to show you something. The bean counters would call it our newest fixed asset. Hello? Anybody home?"

Bill was still contemplating death by snakebite, while the truck bounced and swerved, picking a trail through a stand of young pines.

Far to the east, out Casey Lee's side window, a pink sun oozed up from behind the Atlantic horizon. It wasn't visible, but it showed on everything facing east, including one side of each tree, the sloping branches, half of every rut in the road, and the pickup's hood, as it turned. All looked as if they'd been sprayed pink over pewter.

Gradually, the trees dropped away, and the truck emerged to climb a gentle, cleared rise and stop before a large, wooden building with its unpainted plank face shimmering pink.

"What do you think?" Casey Lee asked. "We built the whole thing ourselves."

They studied the building through the windshield.

"Come on."

As Bill got out, he asked, "You and Penny?"

"Yeah. Penny can sure beat a nail."

They walked to the large double doors. "You'll find she's a lifesaver." Casey Lee fished a key from a ring and opened a large padlock.

"We got a couple guys on the payroll who work for us. They helped. You'll meet 'em. Tray was out here and helped some, too."

"Nice job," Bill commented. "Big. What do we need with a barn?"

Casey Lee slid open one door, while Bill did the other.

"Tell the truth, it's sort of a goof-up. Come in. I was gonna put the office here on the ground floor. We were already under construction when Tray came up with the offer on the double-wide, so we went that route. Worked out great. We got the desks with the deal and had an office near the road. Didn't really need one way out here, and we got the barn we needed."

Bill turned in a slow circle, seeing harvesting and fertilizing equipment, stacks of bagged fertilizer on pallets, and chemicals in drums. A small chemistry lab was shielded from the rest of the room by a ladder built against the wall.

"I got a lot to learn, haven't I, Casey Lee?"

"Least you know it. Lot of these growers been at it their whole lives and don't know shit. Worse, they don't know they don't know."

"What's up above?"

"I'll show you." He flicked a switch, and up on the ceiling above the ladder, light leaked from around a door-sized wooden hatch.

Casey Lee, climbing up first, pushed the weighted plate aside. As Bill followed, Casey Lee stepped to the front of the loft and opened the big wooden shutters. Half the size of the main barn doors and directly above them, they provided exterior access for loading and unloading the loft. Overhead an I-beam ran the length of the peaked roof, extending out over the front doors another ten feet. Hanging from the beam at the far interior end, opposite the opening, was a heavy-duty electric come-along with block and tackle.

The east side of the room was completely empty. On the west side were countless gray metal pots in rows from wall to wall, so close together there wasn't room to walk between.

Bill sniffed the air.

"Stack heaters," Casey Lee said, "fired with Bunker C. That's oil."

"Jesus. How many are there?"

"Not enough. If a grove needs heat, it takes thirty-five or more per acre. We don't have 100,000. I can tell you that."

"What's the worst temperature fruit can survive?"

"At no less than twenty-eight degrees, maybe four or five hours maximum. After that, there's damage. How much depends on how bad it gets. Our enemies are freeze, frost, and hurricanes, not to mention leached-out soil, pests, disease, drought, poor drainage, flood, and now the Greening disease."

Casey Lee stood in the open loft doorway in a swath of bright morning light that cut across the floor and up the northwest corner behind him.

"Take a look."

Bill stepped forward, and their paired shadows bobbed and weaved behind them when they moved. He shielded his eyes with one hand.

From their twenty-odd feet of elevation, he looked over part of what could make or break the rest of his life—endless patch quilts of citrus groves, armadas of trees. The picture was slightly fuzzy with threads of morning mist near the ground. It looked organized, calm, and beautiful, but it was also frightening because there was so much of it. The land was unbelievably flat. The horizon refused to bend even when Bill's eyes followed the tree line.

Something brought his gaze back to directly below. A hundred-yard-wide plot of land ran straight from the front of the barn south for several thousand yards, like football fields laid end-to-end until they disappeared into the haze. The field was shielded on both sides by long rows of tall Australian pines. Between them were planted endless rows of tiny, one-foot-tall bushy plants, each with a shiny white plastic boot around its stem.

"Are those next year's champions?" he asked.

"Actually, yeah. I hope so. They're young budded citrus trees, budlings, by shield budding onto a strong, high-quality stock. When we replace in the grove with one of those, it's called a reset. They usually come from nurseries, but we're doing a little research of our own. I'll show you down on the ground.

"This place's kinda famous, by the way, at least with us. Out there in the middle is where that airplane sat down. I know you heard about the big ol' plane coming in here. Flat scared the shit outta me when I saw it. I thought it was your daddy's, but I got the response on that in no uncertain terms.

"It turned out some guys had engine trouble and landed the son of a bitch in here at night. Tray kind of knew 'em, and got 'em fixed up finally, then they flew out. They tore the shit out of a few rows of our budlings, though."

"Did you call the police?"

Casey Lee smiled without enthusiasm and kicked the edge of the doorway. "I would have, but..."

"Tray Robertson."

"He's like a big brother to me. His daddy, Trent Robertson, raised me, OK?" He closed and pinned the loft doors before walking toward the ladder.

"I'd like to meet Trent Robertson."

"I got a feeling you will." He climbed down the ladder.

At the bottom, he looked up, listening to Bill walk around on the empty wooden floor.

"Bill?"

"Yeah?" Coming to the top of the ladder, he started down. "What's the other side of the loft used for?"

"Nothing so far. This is only the second time I've been up there since it was finished. Why?"

Bill stepped off the end of the ladder and brushed dust off his hands. "It's been swept up as neat as a pin. You can see the broom marks."

"Our boys are pretty good that way. These places get to be a mess in a hurry. You ready?"

"Yeah."

*   *   *

Bill's new mentor worked manual labor most of his life and had the coarse hands and muscle for it. He set a mean pace.

They started with the nursery grove between the Australian pines in front of the barn. They got down on their hands and knees. Apparently, Bill's education would start from the ground up.

Casey Lee hurled information at him, explaining how a stock seedling propagated from seed, then was quarantined, recorded, and logged to assure its variety and family, whether that was sour orange, sweet orange, or trifoliate orange, which was the most cold resistant. Bill saw how rootstock was grown to half an inch in diameter and was budded to the scion, the producer tree that would actually grow the stock.

With Bill on all fours, he watched Casey Lee peel back the protective wrap of a budling to show the graft. Six inches above ground, a small, inverted T-shaped cut was made through the bark. The bud shield, containing the bud from the desired scion, was slipped into the incision so that cambium, the cellular tissue under the bark, abutted against cambium.

"In a month, if the union takes, you cut the stock off above the bud," he explained, "giving you one commercial citrus tree."

Bill stood, shaking his head at his own ignorance. "You know all this shit, don't you?"

"Graduated from Rolling R Ranch, my alma mater, under Professor Trent Robertson, a very enthusiastic and dedicated teacher. It's time to put it on the road, Boy."

Bill recalled his dad saying, *they are worthy because it's the land they were born on.*

"Let's get it on, Bull. We need to hustle."

A minute later, they were banging over a trail road alongside a large grove. Bill looked at Casey Lee's mileage and saw it was at a fat 2,000. The vehicle looked and rode like it was twenty-years old, but it was only one-year old.

Casey Lee, pulling off at an irrigation ditch, put the front end into a soft, sandy mound, scooped up and recently left when the dragline cleared the ditches. Vegetation had already covered it, faster than anything Bill had seen.

In the adjacent grove, the boys were doing what Casey Lee called "acid-sugar tests." He introduced Bill, who heard the others mumbling "Bull" this, and "Bull" that. He hoped they weren't too disappointed.

They were taking cross-section samples of the acid and sugar content in the fruit.

"Fall was unusually warm and wet," Casey Lee explained. "Some fruit is harvestable, but some is still green. The trick is picking at the right time and not to get greedy and stupid. If it looks good but is too early, or vice versa, the state inspectors at the packing house who do the certified acid-sugar tests can reject entire truckloads up to thirty-four percent of a crop. With that much volume being rejected, you can't get a buyer even for cattle feed. Before we pick and haul, I want to know what we got." He waved Bill closer to see how the tests were done.

Trees at the corners of a boxed-in area were flagged. A diagonal was struck, and each tree on it marked. A sample was pulled from selected fruit along the diagonal and tested for acid and soluble solids, or sugar.

"This gives us a good idea of the grove's maturity level," he continued. "Then we can hold, spot pick, or clean pick it all."

After another thrill ride through sand and dust, Casey Lee stopped the truck in the middle of the road, gesturing for Bill to get out, too. They walked into a beautiful pink seedless grapefruit grove.

Casey Lee stopped at one tree, then another, crouching to run his hands over the bark, studying the trunk and foot, feeling the crotch, touching scaffold limbs, and checking the leaves. He occasionally picked fruit from a tree and sliced it open with his fruit knife to taste and smell.

"What're we doing?" Bill asked.

"You have to be out here, walking the groves, always looking for disease, pests, and damage. You look for die back, gummosis, blight, foot rot, root rot, or their symptoms, and, of course, greening. Ants love trees that are sick from a wound or nick. Termites love the ants. Then there's viral infections, like psorosis, tristeza, exocortis, and xyloporosis. How about that word from a Cracker's mouth, eh, Boy? There's one bacterial disease they say is finally gone, called citrus canker. Maybe. Now we've got greening."

They continued their hectic pace until after lunchtime. Bill felt like it had been hours earlier when he saw tractors and trucks stop working, and the men open coolers and bottles before unwrapping sandwiches.

None of that fazed Casey Lee. He charged on, the truck bouncing, diving, and throwing dirt, and Bill tried to keep up. They continued through afternoon, until shadows from the tree canopies crawled up the trunks of the ones across the rows.

Casey Lee noticed with silent approval that the rich man's kid from Yankee Land stayed with him all the way. He never fainted, complained about the heat or dust, and was willing to trudge down row after row in grove after grove, as if he couldn't learn fast enough.

Casey Lee wanted to leap into the air, sail his hat across the road, drop to his knees and offer thanks to God Almighty. He never would say it aloud, but he thought it: *This day is one beautiful attaboy if there ever was one, my Yankee friend.* Instead, he had to turn his back and roll his eyes toward the dying sky in joy.

Although Bill had fourteen months of physical therapy, not even fourteen years could have prepared him for that day. He needed a younger, stronger body, with gator hide instead of skin and claws for hands. He also needed boots and a wide, airy hat.

One of the workers in Burton Groves later estimated that the two bosses covered nearly twenty-five miles on foot that day.

Bill wished he'd been born in that caving-in, smothering grit, the Ashtabula sand, as the locals called it, that shit sand with those shit trees and their shit-sun colored balls, not just to build up the strength but to have the time to learn it all. There were 300,000 trees around him with more to come.

Suddenly, in the time it took to exhale, everything changed in the groves, and the day was over. Trudging down endless rows stopped, as did the CB radios and diesel engines. The men took deep breaths and released, pouring water over their heads before wiping their faces with bandanas and squatting down Indian style to push back their hats. Some lit cigarettes, some dipped from cans or chewed.

Bill's head hung down, and he softly whispered a single word no one else heard. "Finally."

Silence swept the groves, as if a squall just ended.

Even the old-timers, as they probably did each day, noted it as if it was a signal, a whistle only they heard, perhaps a distant train passing at the same time each evening. It was as if the land was being wrested from Man, who was granted its use during the day, and given back to the savannahs for the night.

Casey Lee warned him it would be a long day. "A long day is a day in a citrus grove."

The alarming quiet spread across the flushed-out crowns of dark, waxy green in endless columns that stood like armies, rod-still in gray and silvery helmets, assembled for night watch. The first thready smoke of night fog wove down between the rows and took the dust, while the pastel bath of pink washed over the golden trees again.

Riding beside Casey Lee in the pickup, Bill decided only a tourist could love the Florida sun. As sunlight splashed into the Gulf of Mexico behind them, Casey Lee applied the brakes firmly, then hard enough to start a controlled skid before stopping. Dust swirled around the truck like miniature tornados. When it cleared, Bill was as glassy-eyed as a drunk, staring out the windshield and reading the name *Burton* endlessly on the sign under the night light on the side of the doublewide.

Casey Lee studied his companion's stupor in the rearview mirror and saw the medium-rare broiled forehead, terminally seared nose, and the distant expression. He abruptly turned to face the Yankee boy and said, "Hey, Bull, having a good time so far?"

CHAPTER SIX
WORSE THAN THE BLACKEST NIGHT

Penny glanced at the office clock and swore. *I'm getting outta here by five tonight if it kills me.*

She stayed late several nights to clean Mr. Burton's office in preparation for his arrival. One night alone, she cleaned the nicer of the two executive desks and had it moved into the office he would use. Unfortunately, Casey Lee used that desk at one time, and, apparently, so had Tray Robertson. The filth, clutter, and disorganization in the desk drawers had her muttering.

Filing, she discovered, was done horizontally. Current files were on top of the desk in various, precarious piles. Noncurrent, meaning old but not old enough to toss out, were chucked flat into a file drawer.

Penny removed all of it. She washed out the desk, interior and drawers, went through every shred of paper in the files, threw out junk, and filed Casey Lee's records and correspondence in his own desk.

The current night, though, she finished at 4:55. Before dashing out the door, she detoured to Casey Lee's office with an envelope in her hand with his name on it. She found it behind the file drawer when cleaning the new desk. She tossed the envelope onto Casey Lee's desktop and asked, "That's you, right?"

Casey Lee, engrossed in the Citrus Manual bulletin on advanced weather service via Telex Penny put in his in-box only minutes earlier, grunted. His feet shifted on the corner of the desktop.

Penny turned to leave, calling over her shoulder, "It's five o'clock, and I'm outta here for once. Night, y'all."

When she reached the outside door, she called, "By the by, I had no idea you and Mr. Burton knew each other from before. You a skydiver, too, Casey Lee?"

The door closed behind her.

Casey Lee, immune to Penny's babble, kept his eyes moving back and forth over the last page of the bulletin until her final words finally echoed through his mind for a second try. That usually happened when she made less sense than usual.

He looked at the envelope on his desk. It was a standard business envelope with *Rolling R Ranch* imprinted on the corner and his name, Casey Lee Christy, penned loosely in longhand across the front.

Opening the envelope, he saw scraps of paper fall to his desk. There were six receipts for rental cars, a hotel bill, and an airline ticket, and restaurants—all with his name on them.

He read his name several times as if he'd never seen it before, until comprehension slowly dawned. Panic crushed his stomach, and suffocating fear took over.

In a heartbeat, fear grew to terror worse than the blackest night of a motherless child in the screaming marsh. Always near the surface of his subconscious, a phrase came roaring back to him. *His name is Daniel Christy. He was...the father.*

*   *   *

Outwardly, fifteen-year-old Casey Lee Christy appeared to have everything a boy could want. He lived "Out West." At least, west of what most people thought of as the real Florida, just north of Lake Okeechobee and south of the Kissimmee River Valley, where the sheet of shallow water started forming the huge Blue Cypress Swamp. That eventually fed into the River of Grass, or the Everglades. Central Florida was mostly wetlands, swamp, or rip grass, scrub palms, tundra, groves and occasional ranchland.

The huge Blue Cypress Swamp was his backyard. He stalked it like a bobcat, slipped through rip grass like a doe, slithered up trees like a cottonmouth. Among the hyacinths that ringed the Blue Cypress, he was brother to the Great Blue Herons in the dawn. He floated on the black pools in moonlight, nostrils flaring, eyes glowing like the nearby gators, their red eyes shining. His eyes were more like a Florida Panther's, piercing but gray, not amber.

"Gray as a coming squall," Ma said.

It was Sunday late afternoon when he got his first taste of murder.

His name was Daniel Christy, the father. Casey Lee always used the term "the father," not to distance himself out of respect for the man, as Ma often did when referred to her pastor, but to avoid using the word "my," as in "my father."

When Casey Lee saw or sensed the man trailing him on high ground, he raked across his trail with a branch or doubled back from live oak to pine to scrub palm and disappeared into one of hundreds of hidden thickets.

The father always halted at the trail's end and babbled about demons only he could see before stumbling off, sticking to high palmetto hammocks after being eluded again.

If Casey Lee was tracked on the edge of the marshlands, he slithered deep into the Blue Cypress where almost no man ever went alone. The father never tried. He stayed clear of the deep swamp, and Casey Lee stayed clear of the father.

Then it happened. He didn't see it happen, but he heard it. He always hung back and checked first before stepping from the cabbage palms into the clearing where his tiny frame home stood.

First came quiet begging. Ma carried hidden coins for church tucked into her bodice. She always refused to give them up. There was the usual whining, then more begging, then yelling and screaming.

It became more violent than before. He heard three dull thuds in quick succession, then silence.

Casey Lee froze. Daniel Christy beat Ma to death and took her seventy cents. The instantaneous silence that followed told him what happened.

He ran.

Above the swamp, the shiny brass afternoon sky flickered lazily past the canopy, moving toward twilight. The distant moan and soft rustle of wind rolling through the circumjacent river of grass began, surrounding the deep swamp, as darkness approached. The wild night music began. Animals hooted, roared, honked, hollered, howled warnings, and gave spasmodic screeching and screaming in syncopation of the night's birth, death, life won, and life lost within the shadows.

The night air above Florida's interior cooled until it matched the coastal air. The wind stopped. Tall grass stood still again. Slowly, the hissing sounds over prey backed off and wafted away. Glass encircled lily pads, and the myriad swarming insects settled down. It wasn't a negotiated peace, though. It was daybreak, born again.

He stepped out of the tall reeds onto the old marl road that ran rod-straight east to west across the flatlands as far as he could see until it dropped below the horizon in heat haze. The road surface was already chalky white and shimmering. He squinted, but neither direction seemed preferable over the other. He looked as far as he had ever traveled in both directions.

"Ma, you're dead now," he muttered. "Now what, Ma?"

Overhead, a tiny V floated in the sky, a red-shouldered hawk gliding with wings spread to catch the gentle easterly. Casey Lee followed.

He had grown up without the word *vengeance*. His wild friends in the Blue Cypress didn't deal in such ideas, which were exclusively Man's. However, as he walked away from the place of his birth for the last time, he felt vengeance gnaw at him, pulling him.

The dark memory, as well as the phrase, never left him. *His name is Daniel Christy...the father.*

CHAPTER SEVEN
FALL, WHEN SPIT DON'T HIT THE SIDEWALK

The whole breathless heartland shimmered like a cane cutter's back. It rained more in less time, built up in the west during the afternoon, and came down in monsoons for twenty minutes. By morning, old-timers said, "Spit don't hit the sidewalk again." Tropical summer bore down, burned on, until folks thought it always would.

"We don't get fall, we get a crap game," Casey Lee told Bill during his first days in the groves. "Remember the Essentials of Citrus, Bull? It's sunlight, heat, cold—we gotta have a cold snap to bring out the color break—and water. This time of year, the so-called essentials can get overdone and kill it all."

Bill couldn't believe how much scientific information he absorbed since he arrived. In the course of any single day, Casey Lee dropped dozens of invaluable nuggets: trees are as susceptible to sunburn as humans; high temperatures cause fruit drop; a cold snap brings color and sweetness; a freeze brings curtains; fifty-two inches of rain is normal, but trees standing in water rot quickly; plus all the complicated treatments for retarding Greening disease.

Casey Lee never let up. "Don't forget the dirty H word, Bull." He whirled to face southwest and pointed like he held a gun. "Hurricane! Bam! Folks can't even say the word around here, Bull. They stick their heads in the sand and never learn."

Casey Lee ridiculed other growers, telling Bill how Hurricane Betsy years earlier ripped through the Bahamas, Florida, and Louisiana, taking a hundred lives and causing one billion dollars in damage.

"To prepare for Billion Dollar Betsy, the growers paced their groves all day, accomplishing nothing, just like they do every fall. They stand around and hope, praying they don't get snake eyes. It's a crap game."

It was true, too. They were trying to beat Mother Nature at her own game.

Those things didn't worry Bill at the moment, though. Suddenly, the only citrus man who wasn't outside pacing was Casey Lee Christy. He disappeared three days earlier, and no one heard a word from him.

He didn't show up for work and wasn't home, either. He had no family, so it wasn't a family crisis. He wasn't dating anyone. Was he injured, sick, or had an accident somewhere?

Did something slip from my Yankee mouth I didn't realize at the time? Bill wondered.

He didn't feel like Bull at all. There was no way to get through the fall harvest alone. Even if everything went well, if it didn't freeze, blow, or fry, he still faced the huge harvest. Big money had been invested in the ground and hung on the trees. It wasn't a time for amateurs.

Bill asked anyone he could, the locals and crew members, about Casey Lee's absence. They just shook their heads. Worse, those who knew him said they'd never seen Casey Lee act strangely before. He was never depressed, and he never even sneezed, let alone got sick with a cold.

Finally, he had a glimmer of an idea when he spoke with Penny, who was also looking for Casey Lee. She called Miss Holly, who seemed closer to Casey Lee than anybody except Trent Robertson. Penny called her "Miss Northern Broom" and felt she was trying to get closer to Casey Lee. It was clear, but Penny knew the woman would never become his lover, because she was a Yankee.

Penny tried to imagine what would happen if she brought home a Yankee and said, "Mama, Daddy, this here's my lover!"

Nevertheless, the woman might know something, so Penny waited for her to return her call.

Bill went to Penny's desk and asked, "Do you have any idea where Casey Lee is?"

She looked up as if expecting him to tell her. "I don't know, Bill. I thought you chewed him out for some damned thing, which sounded surprising, since you two were such good buddies and all. Shoot, you're the boss. You can chew out anybody you want. Don't make no never mind to me."

"What old buddies?"

"You and Casey Lee was skydiving buddies, Silly. That surprised me, too, I'll tell you. Talk about opposites. When I came across all his receipts for his trip last year, I gave them to him. I found them when I cleaned out your desk before your arrival. They were in an envelope, as I recall, from Rolling R Ranch, with Casey Lee's name on it. I figured he was saving them, so I dumped them on his desk."

"What did he say?"

"Nothing. I was on my way out the door. I said something about not knowing you two were old friends, and..."

"What did he say?"

"Not the first thing. I was out the door by then. What's this got to do with...?"

"Probably nothing. May I see those receipts?"

"You'd have to ask Casey Lee, Sir. All I did was look to see if it needed junking or filing."

Bill leaned over the desk. "Penny, it's important. You have to remember what the receipts were for."

Suddenly, she became frightened. "OK, Mr. Burton, Sir." Her expression showed she thought he was acting crazy. "One for a rental car in New York. Another for an airline ticket round trip from here...well, from West Palm Beach to New York. One other, which was why I thought he visited you, to some skydiving place in some county in Connecticut."

"Fairfield?" He spelled the name. "Was it Fairfield County? Skydive?"

"What?"

"S-K-Y-D-I-V-E."

"Could be. Skydive, Inc., Fairfield County? Yeah, I think that was it."

"What did it say? Was it a sales slip for lessons?"

"Mr. Burton, I didn't care a hoot. It took place before I started here. I only thought it was pieces of paper that might need filing or tossing. I thought I was doing my job, trying to turn this place into an office. Now you've got me upset."

"Penny, I'm sorry, but this could be important. Please, what was on that Skydive receipt?"

"It was like a sales slip. It had *Rental* scribbled on it, and two letters above, like A and B, but not those letters."

"H and C?" He leaned over and wrote the letters upside down on her pad.

"Yeah. What's that?"

"Harness and parachute. It means he rented a harness and parachute."

Penny looked up at him. "You boys have a ball, did ya?"

Standing up straight, he looked across the office to the trees outside, then beyond. His memory opened, and he saw a parachute stretched out on the long metal table in the Skydive parachute loft in Fairfield County, Connecticut. He heard his own voice from the TV show, *The skydiver is responsible for his own equipment.*

"Mr. Burton? You all right?"

"I...I'm fine, Penny."

The phone rang, and Penny caught it on the first ring. "Oh. All right. Mary Beth it is, then. This is Penny from Burton Groves. Do you have any inclination where Casey Lee might be?"

"I might. Let me speak with Mr. Burton." She didn't even say *adios.*

Penny was upset by the lack of manners. "Well, now. Just a New York minute. I'll have to see if the boy is in."

Bill quickly stepped into his office. Penny heard him pick up his phone and knew she should hang up, but she decided to wait until she was absolutely sure the call went through. Besides, the thin walls made listening to her boss easy. She'd set down the receiver in a second or two.

"Bill Burton, here."

"Mr. Burton, this is Mary Beth Holly."

"Yes, Miss Holly. What can I do for you?"

"Well, this is quite forward of me, and I hope you'll forgive me, but could you have dinner with me this evening at my home?"

"Dinner, Miss Holly?" Bill jumped when he heard something drop and break in the outside office. "Your house?"

"Please, call me Mary Beth. It's Bill, isn't it? It's important, Bill. There will be one other party joining us, to protect you from me if you're frightened."

"Don't be silly. Who?"

"Mr. Robertson."

"Tray Robertson?"

"No, not Tray. His father, Trent Robertson, will be here."

He paused. "Miss Holly, may I ask what this is all about?"

"Yes, you may. Shall we say six-thirtyish?"

★   ★   ★

Penny spent the rest of the afternoon pouting over her sweet new Yankee boss taking up with the skinny Yankee schoolmarm.

"You gonna lay an Eddie Arnold on her, aren't ya?" she asked Bill.

"Who?"

"He's a Grand Ol' Opry star who sang country or pop, not hillbilly or honky tonk. He was loved by everybody, not just Southerners. He always looked pretty, even when he didn't feel pretty. With those silver tones, there wasn't a song or anything else he couldn't sell." She sighed. "He can flat do a number on a person."

Bill was still confused.

"Around here, when a guy's basically a no-good redneck shitkicker, but he looks and acts like a nice guy, he's doin' an Eddie Arnold on ya. He either wants to sell you something or date your daughter."

Penny also offered advice on what he should wear, including the pros and cons of a necktie for a dinner date. "Even that stuck-up Yankee schoolmarm, who's too old for either of you boys, by the way, wouldn't insist on a necktie in this weather."

Bill had a new Western belt with silver buckle that was size 28-30 compared to his 34s from Darien. He walked an average of ten to fifteen miles a day working, and he looked it.

A clean shave, with his short brown hair, good cheekbones, and taut tan skin made him a clean package. He wore his pressed blue blazer over a crisp, short-sleeved white button-down shirt, and new western-cut khakis and new polished boots. He had the right appearance to do an Eddie Arnold.

He walked up the walkway to the address Penny provided, a rare, framed, two-story Old Florida home circa 1920, with a double-deck porch across the front and both sides. The old home was freshly painted with a crisp, glistening white and had been lovingly restored. The entrance was bordered by a hibiscus hedge bursting in strawberry-colored blossoms.

The house faced east directly on the mainland shore of the Indian River within the fishing village of Sebastian in northern Indian River County. It overlooked the river, which everyone had to learn wasn't really a river but a long saltwater estuary running north and south between the mainland and the barrier islands.

At Sebastian, from the mainland to the ocean inlet, the estuary was nearly two miles wide.

He could imagine the scene a quarter century earlier and how Old Florida used to be. It should have made him feel cool, but all he had going for him was the Eddie Arnold, which worked only on the outside of a person. He stared at the doorbell button with his mouth as dry as the first time he strapped on a parachute.

"Bull Burton!" Mary Beth blurted with a magnificent smile when she answered. She opened the screen. "I've heard so much about you, I feel as if I already know you. Come in."

He brushed past her. She was tall, and he hoped she missed his expression at the front door, when he almost puked out of nerves.

"May I call you Bill, Bull?"

He tried not to stare at such a lovely woman. "Bill, please. Yes, call me Bill."

"Drink?" she turned to the little bar across the room.

"Yes. Scotch and soda?"

"Fine."

Her blonde hair was pulled back and held in place by a white scarf. A delicate gold chain danced on her neck above a red scoop-neck sleeveless shell that matched the hibiscus out front. It was tucked into a white Lily Pulitzer skirt slit to above the knee in back, very chic.

While she poured, she asked, "Well, what do you think?"

Gorgeous, he thought, though he restrained himself from saying it. Suddenly, not being an instant bore seemed important.

She whirled with two short glasses on cocktail napkins and caught his eye. Looking at him from under her lashes, she extended a drink.

"What do you think about the house?" she asked. "We tried to give it a contemporary look without destroying the antiquity of the place. Welcome, and just in time, I might add."

"Thank you. Cheers. *Just in time?* he wondered. "You said we?"

"I'm sorry?"

"You said we tried to give it a contemporary look."

"Trent and I. Trent's a master carpenter and cabinetmaker. It's his hobby. I hired him, but he said he just wanted to do it. He loves these old homes. Please, come sit down and relax."

They moved to the living area overlooking the Indian River.

The ground floor was one open room, leaving only the kitchen enclosed. The living area was contemporary and airy. Decorated in subtle, cool, colorful but muted Caribbean shades and comfortable furnishings, it was somehow casual and sophisticated simultaneously, but still remained thoroughly Southern. The original cypress walls and floors remained, but they were sanded smooth, bleached and pickled. Overhead, ceiling fans turned slowly.

"I'm in a room on the beach so far."

"Maybe we can help. Trent knows all the spots."

"May I ask...?"

"He'll be right down." Looking toward the staircase, she called, "Trent? Mr. Burton is here."

She hadn't wasted any time calling Trent the day after her disastrous, foreshortened date with Tray, saying she felt much better. Her voice was cheery, and she just blurted, "Do you know this Roosevelt Awbrey friend of his?"

Trent claimed he never met the man.

"Did you know Tray's trying to get Casey Lee a job at Burton Groves?"

There was a pause. She wondered if he set down the receiver or shifted it to the other ear.

"I know it's none of my business," she continued, "but I have the feeling Casey Lee might be the last to know."

"Well, the idea might have been mentioned in passing. It's certainly the sort of thing that could be good experience." He abruptly cleared his throat and asked, "May I stop over?"

★　★　★

When Trent arrived, Mary Beth's mouth hung open for nearly an hour, as he unloaded the nightmare of what was happening right under her nose in her adopted land of Central Florida.

A few days later, she had to contend with Bill Burton standing in front of her.

Bill wanted to ask what the hell was going on, but he was determined to play it Mary Beth's way and go along with cocktail conversation for a while.

The stairs moaned and squeaked with the weight of Trent Robertson, trim for what had to be 200 pounds and sixtyish looking, impressive in a sport shirt and gray slacks. He came bounding down with his hand out and his feet bare.

"Burton!" Trent said. "By golly, you're a sight. We're delighted you could come."

"Thank you, Sir. It's nice to be here."

Mary Beth slipped to the bar. "Drink, Trent?"

"Bourbon, Woman. Bourbon. Aren't they cute at that age, Bill? I'll tell ya, you sure are something. Casey Lee told me about your accident. You all right now?"

"Fine, more or less."

"No cane or anything?"

"No cane, just a wedge in one shoe. I'm jealous of you. I can't run around barefoot as well anymore."

"Mary Beth, where the hell are my boots?" He accepted the drink she offered.

"I believe you set them outside," she said. "They had cattle auction on them, remember?"

She glanced at Bill as if reading his mind. He assumed that she, approximately his age, and Trent, at sixty-one, were playing house, which he doubted was the impression she wanted to convey to her guest.

"Trent, will you please *tell* Mr. Burton?" she asked.

The small talk was apparently over.

"Sorry. Of course." Trent's mood became deadly serious. "We spread the receipts out on this coffee table last night. Casey Lee was here, and we looked them over, as well as the envelope with his name on it. Mary Beth had him try to duplicate the signature at least twenty times. He couldn't come close."

"His penmanship is terrible," she added. "I never thought I'd be happy to say that."

"But anyone could have scrawled his name," Trent continued. "Mary Beth wrote down the dates, times, and flight numbers from the airline ticket. The spent ticket showed the return flight from New York arrived at West Palm Beach International early in the evening on June fifth."

Bill, who was extremely familiar with that date, managed not to flinch.

"Casey Lee Christy was with me that day." Trent looked up, his eyes glistening. "We exercised a couple of the horses, rode a western fence at the ranch, and had one of our usual talks. He told me he'd been on the phone with your daddy in Connecticut earlier that day. That's how I remembered. Your accident had just happened. He and Mr. Dick Burton cried on the phone. That evening, Casey Lee was with me in my den going over personal affairs. I remember the evening distinctly."

★   ★   ★

Casey Lee listened to every word. After they handed off their horses, they talked for hours. The boss told Casey Lee about the changes to his will. He placed the ranch in trust with the bank, so Tray would never gain control.

"I don't understand him," he admitted to his stepson, feeling total disappointment in his own son. "Tray's a hothead with terrible judgment. He knows it all. How did that happen?"

"What's the trouble, Boss Man. Where's he now?"

"I told him I was taking you to South America to look at cattle. He insisted on going, flew down this past week, or I think so. He could have gone anywhere—Texas, Paris, or the moon. I've lost all understanding of him."

Trent looked up, searching the boy's face for support.

Trent regarded Bill and Mary Beth in sincere belief. "Casey Lee never used the airline ticket. I swear it."

"Has he ever been out of Florida, Trent?" Mary Beth asked.

"Never."

Bill sat back in his chair and said quietly, "I just found out about those receipts myself. There's no reason to doubt you, Mr. Robertson. I don't know what's going on, but I think it's time for the police, don't you?"

"No!" Trent snapped, then turned apologetic. "Casey Lee is like my own son. Isn't he, Mary Beth? He was half crazy when he walked in here last night."

"We had to prove to him that he didn't do it," Mary Beth added. "He thought he'd lost his mind, that he'd gone to Connecticut without remembering it. We even considered he'd been drugged until we put it all together and realized he was here at that time."

"Look," Trent began, "he'll be at the office tomorrow morning. Meet him, please. If I were you, I'd just pick things up from there and go. He's hurt. He's a Cracker—you know. He'd never mention it directly, but he's been accused, and he's innocent. In fact, he's in as much danger as you are. He's like my own flesh and blood. I've loved him since he was a boy. You should have seen him the day he stumbled barefoot onto my ranch. He really showed us a thing or two. You had to see that little fella to believe it."

★　★　★

"Hey, Boy," the tall rancher with curly white hair, a white mustache, sky-blue eyes, and topped by a stained Stetson, looked down at the barefoot boy, who had his jaw set and looked right back at him. "You big enough to ride a horse?"

"Believe I can ride that one." He nodded at a skittish black-and-white stallion kicking up dust all over the corral. The horse had a single bit and bridle, with long training reins dragging on the ground.

There were over forty horses on the Rolling R, but in the corral, there was only one. The ranch hands hanging around seemed to prefer staying out of that corral, too.

"The pinto? Well, now, he's not quite ready for a real cowboy like you yet, Boy."

The boy was already over the top rail of the fence and easing up toward the horse from behind. Wheezing half-heartedly, the pinto swung his head back to look at the intruder from the corner of his eye, while the black tail flicked lazily against one flank.

Motionless, Casey Lee made the high-pitched sound of a cattle egret. "Kra-ack. Kra-ack. Kra-ack."

"That oughta bring him to his knees, right, Boys?" the boss ridiculed to the delight of the hands who stood watching, their elbows on the rail.

"Ever break a wild-ass bronc with a bird call, Roy?" one hand called.

"Shee-it," was the answer.

The boy looked like he hadn't heard that one before. Twelve hands stopped working and came to the fence to watch.

The stallion lumbered around to catch up with the direction of his head. He looked at the boy straight on, bobbed his head, and snorted gently.

He had a white star on an otherwise black forehead, and he was black all the way down his throat and chest and the front of each leg. The backs of his legs were white. On his back was a white saddle pattern over his black coat.

The boy lifted his right palm slowly and chanted so softly only the horse could hear, using the Muskogee Seminole dialect, "*Micowakasassa, Micanopy, Micowakasassa.*" He acknowledged to the paint that the animal was chief of all chiefs of all herds.

The horse lumbered up to the boy and pawed the dust. The hands leaning against the fence muttered in disbelief.

The boy gathered the reins easily, patted the black nose, and whispered another Indian phrase. "*Ishtohollo. Istohollo. Ishtohollo.*" He inched calmly and gently alongside the horse and stopped beside its ribs, stroking its barrel gently just ahead of the belly.

The steed acknowledged the touch with a faint wheeze.

The boy flicked the left rein over the horse's neck so it hung down over the withers on the right. He slithered under the black cheek and muzzle on the horse's side and stepped back. Clenching his right hand hard, he held it up to the steed and whispered, *"Ishtoholl, Micanopy!"*

In a flashing high jump, the boy leaped to its back and let his legs envelope the animal. There he was, bareback, high on the horse's natural saddle.

The horse snorted, then bobbed its head in delight. The cowhands, all straddling the top rail by then, almost fell off in shock.

"Micowakasassa," he praised the horse, then spoke to the boss. "Could you open the gate?"

"What the hell you saying to that critter, Boy?" the boss obliged.

"I gave him a choice—walk out or jump the fence."

"And he simply decided to walk out, did he?"

"Not at first. I had to remind him who he was."

The pinto, with the boy on its back, stepped forward into a fenced grazing pasture. The boy patted the horse, said something, and hugged him quickly with his legs. The horse took off.

They dived down the pasture until they were in a full gallop. When they reached a small, scattered herd of Santa Gertrudis cattle, they circled them, stopped and balked, cut and darted, gathering the cows and calves into a tight knot and scattering the white cattle egrets. Then they trotted back.

When the two reached the crowd of cowboys at the gate, the boys shook their heads in disbelief. They hollered and spat, while some threw their hats in the dirt and stomped them. The ones on the top rail of the corral fence almost kicked it down with their heels. A couple even nodded and winked at the boy.

"I meant," the boss said, poking a brown saddle resting on the fence, "could you ride him wearing one of these?"

"I recall you asked if I could ride this horse."

"Can you break him to saddle, Boy?"

"You hiring?"

The boss laughed. "What the hell's your name, Son?"

"The name's Casey Lee Christy, from out of east of here. What's yours, beggin' your pardon, Sir?"

"Name's Trent Robertson, and this here you're on is the Rolling R Ranch."

"Much obliged, Mista Robertson."

Trent instinctively liked something about the boy. "Guess I'll have to put you to work, Boy. Somebody's got to break that wild paint." He glanced at the boy in mock distaste.

"If I break him, he's mine."

"Now see here, Young'un. I'll do the..."

"He won't allow a hand on him but me, as you already know. If he don't get broke, what good is he to you?"

The boss leaned against the corral fence, crossed his legs, pulled his hat down, crossed his arms, and studied the boy. He squinted his experienced eyes as if seeing something pleasant but rare, something that was always in short supply.

"It's a deal, Son."

Casey Lee stuck out his hand and mumbled, "*Ishtohollo.*"

"What's that?"

"'Mighty good,' Mista Robertson. Oh, by the way, how much citrus we got on the Rolling R?" For the first time in Casey Lee's fifteen years, he felt good, even happy. He never knew what feeling good was like. He'd been busy just trying to stay alive, and that was becoming easier.

Thanks to Trent Robertson, the cowhands, and Mr. Robertson's son, Tray—though he wasn't around that much, being nine years older and a man—everything was different.

Whenever Roy was asked about Tray's whereabouts, he said, "Busy in town." Roy, the foreman of the Rolling R, fifth biggest spread of its kind in the State of Florida, always knew where everybody was. He was Trent's longest-term employee.

"Fuckin' his brains out, that's where," someone in the bunkhouse said, assuming Casey Lee was out of earshot, because the boss told all of them to watch their language around him.

"Aw, don't listen to that filth, Son," Roy said. "Young Mister Tray has dates with girls, of course. Besides, he's very busy with the business end of things."

It was quickly pointed out that Tray, at twenty-four, was the youngest President in the history of the Florida Cattleman's Association. He was friends with the folks at Texas' King Ranch and had, with their blessing, introduced the Santa Gertrudas breed into Florida.

A lot of the rolling-eyes-and-spit-tobacco-juice crowd around the ranch said that wasn't the half of it, though.

"The fucker's a flat-out standin' up stud machine, Shee-it!"

Roy hushed the men. "You're full of shit, too."

Casey Lee had heard the word the first day he'd arrived, and he practiced it until he had the inflection perfect.

Late one afternoon, Tray had Casey Lee shine his fancy alligator boots for him. He'd never seen anything like them before. They came in a box in the mail, a gift from the King Ranch in Texas, the biggest ranch in America, where Tray said Santa Gertrudas cattle originated. He claimed the King Ranch people were friends of his.

Casey Lee put the final brushings to the shiny pointed toes that looked like the skin of a Black Indigo snake.

"I've got a big date," Tray said, winking.

Casey Lee looked up and winked back, showing he understood such things.

He was growing up and had a fair idea of what might be involved in a date. He also had a hero. The trouble was, beyond that point, he couldn't get close to Tray. It seemed like they might be getting close when Tray helped him learn the citrus business. Tray knew it backward and forward and hated it, but Casey Lee stayed on his heels, and Tray eventually became enthusiastic about some aspect of growing fruit.

Generally, Tray avoided the boy, as he did the hands who worked the cattle.

Roy told Casey Lee, "A man in Tray's position can't pal around with a bunch of redneck cowhands. He has to mix with politicians, real-estate people, and bankers—all those do-gooders."

Still, Casey Lee stood as close to Tray as he could, trying to listen when he spoke.

"Taxes and the changes in the tax laws will ruin Florida agriculture," Trent said.

"People buy up groves and never see 'em again," Roy said. "They call 'em shelters."

Tray cursed and walked away. "I don't give a goddamn. It's good for grove real estate."

Casey Lee wondered how anyplace could give you shelter if you weren't there.

Then there was pressure on what Tray called the Greenbelt Laws, the special way agricultural real estate was assessed.

"Tray has lunch with the politicians over that one," Roy said.

People who lived east of them were sometimes as densely populated as 300 to the acre, and each one had a vote. A rancher or grower had only one vote.

Then there was a time when Tray wasn't around at all. He seemed to age and pulled away from his younger stepbrother with each revelation.

Casey Lee did his ranch chores and learned the citrus and cattle businesses, two endeavors he was determined to master. Adjacent to orange and grapefruit groves, the Rolling R Ranch had a couple acres of resets, new little trees being raised to fill in where trees were removed due to damage, age, disease, or the deadly Greening. Casey Lee's citrus education began there.

He learned that right where he stood, at almost exactly 27.5 degrees north latitude, was the finest place in the world to grow citrus.

"It's because of the climate," the harvesting manager explained. "It's tropical enough to be warm and humid in the summer, cool with a touch of frost in winter. The balance of those temperatures maintains the balance of sugar and acid in Florida fruit, which is considered the sweetest-tasting in the U.S.

"The quality of the fruit is directly related to the latitude at which it is grown. As far as we're concerned, this is where the tropics begin."

Always there to chime in or sharpen the focus, Trent Robertson said, "You can grow better fruit at a higher latitude, but there's the greater threat of a serious freeze. All of that means we can't just pick up and move up or down the road 100 miles. We're out of business if we lose our location, so we have to take care of it—water, land, and air. It's all we got, Son. It's more than somebody saying, '27.5 north latitude is where the tropics begin.'"

★　★　★

In fall, they had bright sun, falling temperatures, and the grapefruit were the size of green baseballs. On southwest exposures, they were lightly tinted bright yellow, just like Tray said. The groves were all groomed, clear, clean, and mowed. There was no foot rot, red scale, black scale, purple scale, no missing nutrients or micronutrients, such as nitrogen, iron, zinc, manganese, phosphorous, potash, magnesium, calcium, copper, or boron. Everything had been done according to the manager's calendar and his continuous soil pH testing. They had no dry rot, tristeza quick decline, gummosis, or gophers. Any tree suffering from greening had been thinned out.

Casey Lee looked forward to his first harvest. For the first time in his life, not counting Ma's tutoring at Blue Cypress, he was in school.

He got up at four in the morning, worked until time for school, then picked up again after he came home in the afternoon.

"He gets his eight hours in," Roy said.

"We need some brains in this outfit," the boss said.

Casey Lee constantly compared himself to everyone he met. He came away feeling the lesser most of the time. It was odd. He was ashamed about being more or less an orphan and clammed up if anyone asked about his family, his coming from the boondocks, the way he talked, or anything else. His bad teeth bothered him. He thought they made him look funny, so he tried to talk with his mouth half closed. He had the Cracker mumbles worse than anyone.

It wasn't so much what others thought. It was what he thought of himself. Knowing he had a long way to go, he sensed somehow that the old man knew intuitively what he was going through.

"You boys seen the fruit in that M-1 grove?" Trent asked. "That's Indian River quality! Your young Mr. Christy's a citrus man, goddamn it. That's one attaboy for you, Fella!"

Casey Lee liked that *attaboy*. He would remember that.

Sometimes, lying in his bunk, he decided that what he felt was probably what it was like to have a real father. It was an unfamiliar bond that was growing between the rancher and himself—Casey Lee's first such relationship.

Eventually, much to Casey Lee's delight, his older brother, Tray, made an about-face and started treating Casey Lee almost like an equal.

Casey Lee figured he was the one who had changed, especially since he turned twenty-one.

★　★　★

Telling all that to Bill left Trent's sad eyes flooded with tears. He stared at the grain of the bare cypress plank floor, while Mary Beth and Bill waited.

"You two are the business," he said finally. "Take charge and get on with it, Boy. I want to see Burton Groves the biggest thing in citrus in this state. We'll get rid of this horror. Believe me. Florida's nothing but ups and downs. I fought scum all my life to get where I am.

"You may think it's no affair of mine, but it is." He raised his hand before the others could speak. "We know your so-called accident may not have been an accident. We know somebody wants you out of the picture and wants Casey Lee out, too, so that person tried to frame him for your expected death.

"We don't know much, but, sooner or later, this will bust open. That's when we'll find out why."

"Bill, trust us a little further and listen, please?" Mary Beth asked.

He looked at her in a new way. She wasn't pleading. She was a strong young woman. As he stared at her, she returned his gaze.

As the evening passed, Bill learned there was plenty more than a threat to his life going on. They gave him validated reports of murder, disappearances, fires, bombings, barns destroyed, abandoned aircraft and trucks—many of them stolen, all up and down the Treasure Coast. As he listened, he saw the white-haired farmer sitting across from him as damaged and disappointed, but he was still a tower of strength. There was something tragic about Trent Robertson.

Mary Beth, sitting at his side, nodded and smiled, sometimes sadly.

"This is a nationwide opioid epidemic, my dear Mr. Burton," Trent said. "It's big-time trafficking and volume, the biggest such trafficking scheme to ever hit Florida. I never saw anything like it before in citrus country.

"Right behind all the illegal immigrants from Eastern Europe, the Caribbean, Central and South America, with their weed, powder drugs, and needles, come the hookers pouring out of Miami to be launched at our citrus tycoons and cowboys. Those boys have never seen anything like it. The rumble in the groves and cattle pastures is on, rolling north to primeval music from South Beach, Miami, Haiti, and Cuba, all led and arranged by the likes of the Columbian mafia.

"Some bigwig dealer obviously flew in to his Miami Beach condo, cruised over the boonies here, and got an idea for how to take the heat off trafficking by boat through Miami ports. He would go airborne and use our sparsely populated flat groves, pastures that are often absentee owned to come in day and night without being detected. Such places are reasonably secure and still close to the markets.

"If you ask me how many natural airstrips are in Indian River, Okeechobee, Brevard, St. Lucie, and Martin Counties, I'd have to say I don't know. I know there are 200,000 acres under citrus cultivation. That might mean 500 possible landing sites. Most of these drug-filled hogs land, unload, and take off without incident. We've counted twenty-two abandoned to date, along with several murders and disappearances of unsuspecting farmers who accidentally walked in on the action. There's so much money involved, the cost of an airplane doesn't matter, nor does human life."

"Tell Bill the figure you have in mind, Trent," Mary Beth said.

"The street take to date could easily total hundreds of millions of dollars."

"They seem to have a preference, though," she added. "They like absentee-owned groves the best."

Trent looked down at his hands. "There's some evidence to indicate that." He looked up and swallowed, choosing his words with care. "Perhaps. There's the possibility, a possible scenario, as they say, that there were payoffs or out-and-out rents paid for the use of certain properties. They had unstated or misstated uses, or maybe the owners didn't even care. Maybe some Mafia goon walked up to their door when certain people needed money. Desperate people don't look before they leap. All I know is, it's the biggest importation of illegal substances in the state's history. There isn't enough law enforcement to handle Miami, let alone out here. I don't know what we'll do. Do you?"

I don't know what to make of a lot of this, Bill thought. "What can the authorities do?"

Trent nodded slowly. "The sheriffs don't have the manpower nor the jurisdiction half the time. There's U.S. Customs, the Bureau of Narcotics and Dangerous Drugs, the DEA, and the FBI. They're on it, but they have no predetermined jurisdiction. The cops don't know where the drugs come from, whether it's out of the country or from a hole in the ground. The Feds are too thin to do much up here, they say. As I said, they're too thin in Miami."

They discussed scenarios, weak links, and rethought old facts and theories through a late dinner, clearing dishes, coffee, and after-dinner liqueur and coffee again.

The meeting was finally over when Trent said, "Mary Beth, will you get my boots? I'd better take them with me."

Mary Beth and Bill stood in the doorway, watching the old rancher trudge slowly to his car, open the door, start the engine, and drive off south along the Indian River.

"This is aging him," Mary Beth said, taking Bill's arm.

They went back inside.

When Bill drove down from Sebastian to his efficiency for a shower, he thought back over the evening. He believed the story about Casey Lee. One call home to Papa Dick could verify that, if Dad could remember Casey Lee's call.

The thought made him chuckle. *Dad would remember a call from Casey Lee, all right,* he thought.

He'd be able to keep the bank appointment. Once again, Bill felt more like Bull again. The so-called accident was something else, though. He'd never felt it was an accident at all.

On a much-nicer note, there was Miss Mary Beth Holly.

CHAPTER EIGHT
A FACE OF RAGE

Treasure Coast Citron Bank opened its doors at nine o'clock the following morning, and they were waiting. Bill learned another lesson in his quest to comprehend a Florida Cracker.

They were not only fiercely proud but resilient. They never said they were sorry and didn't know how to act if an outsider said that to them, yet they didn't shrug off anything. They'd rather die than say, "Oh, that's all right. It was my fault." If someone belabored an apology to set things right, an inimitable blank look put the onus of guilt where it belonged—on the apologist. From then on, the incident was, "Ain't worth the words to describe it." It was over without any grudges. They'd never call a friend a "friend," but they'd do anything to show it.

"Remember," Casey Lee told Bill, "you're Bull Burton. You're what he thinks you are. He wants to call you Bull. It'll make him feel like a big shot, one of the boys, a cog in the wheel of local progress. Why, just knowing you could put him in the Rotary Club. You know that, Bull? Remember, you don't beg for the loan, but you might be willing to share an opportunity. His name is Arthur Wendell Ryan. He likes to be called Arthur, but I believe his mother calls him Wendell. She's had him under control from day one. He's twenty-four. Let's get it on."

The President and Vice President of Burton Groves, Incorporated, sauntered through the bank doors, introduced themselves to a guard, and entered the well-furnished but surgically clean private office of Assistant Vice President and Commercial Loan Officer A. W. Ryan.

"Bull Burton!" Ryan bellowed for all to hear, shaking Bill's hand profusely. "Welcome to Citron."

Bill expected Casey Lee to say, "And the same to you, Kid," when Casey Lee offered his hand, and the bank officer ignored it, but he remained silent.

"We're so pleased that you've selected us to be of service. We strongly feel you'll be one of the great names in Florida citrus in our community."

"Thank you, Mr. Ryan," Bill said, gesturing to Casey Lee.

"Please call me Arthur, Bull."

"My associate, Casey Lee Christy."

"Of course." Ryan gave an impatient gesture. "Sit down, Gentlemen."

The young assistant vice president wore an indigo-blue, three-piece, polyester cotton suit with light pin stripes. Under his vest was a white, tab-collared shirt with redundant gold collar pin. His full head of dark hair covered his ears, and his pink face came from standing outside during his lunch hour, hoping to catch some sun.

Casey Lee reconnoitered that as part of his banker-selection process. "When Yankee kids come down here to their fancy jobs, fresh out of college, they have a hard time remembering they aren't on spring break from school anymore."

Bill sat and looked powerful, as Casey Lee described it, with his legs crossed to show his boots. Casey Lee insisted he buy expensive, handmade gator boots to go with his buttoned-up collar and bolo tie. Bill eyed Ryan and wondered, with all the possible bankers to choose from, how he won the toss.

"Well now." Ryan took a file from his desktop drawer and placed it before him. There was nothing else on the desktop, not even a notepad, except, of course, his nameplate.

"Everything seems to be in order. Bull, I saw you on TV when you were in New York."

Casey Lee nodded in amazement of Bill's good fortune.

"Enjoy it?" Bill asked, though he didn't enjoy it himself.

"That was so cool, Boy, I tell you."

"Should I be signing anything while we talk, Mr. Ryan?"

"And now looky here," Casey Lee added. "Here he is right in front of you, in the flesh."

"Well, yes, right in front of me. I mean..." Ryan turned the file around. "You can sign where you see the red X's, if you will."

Ryan sat back and folded his hands. "I'm pleased to say that I—the bank, that is—agree to a firm commitment of the full amount to accommodate your transaction, as per your application, payable at closing, which I suggest be held right here, if that's convenient."

"Fine, Mr. Ryan, and thank you." Bill set down the pen and pushed the folder back toward the lender.

"Bull, I want you to call me Arthur. My pleasure." With a knowing wink, he confided, "You came very well recommended, I might add."

Casey Lee perked up.

"That's nice," Bill said. "Who was it?"

"Mr. Robertson sent a very nice letter."

"Good ol' Trent?" Casey Lee asked innocently.

'Heavens, no," Ryan said in dismay. "Not the old man. He's retired, out of the picture. I meant Tray Robertson. He runs the big Rolling R Ranch, you know, a big operation. He's an up-and-coming power around here, too."

Casey Lee looked mesmerized.

"In fact, my political action group, all of us young professionals here in the county—what the heck, we'll be running the state soon enough, right?—are considering Mr. Tray Robertson for public office, maybe senator or governor."

Until that moment, Bill hadn't fully grasped Tray's status in the local power structure.

Casey Lee, however, wasn't surprised. He jumped right in. "Wonderful. Great thinking, Wendell. Progress. I can smell it from here. Yes, Sir."

"Well thank you, Mr...?"

"Christy, Wendell. Casey Lee Christy."

"And it's Arthur. Wendell's just my middle name."

Casey Lee's grin was almost ear to ear. "Your mother's maiden name, huh?"

*   *   *

When they were outside, walking toward the Jeep, Bill asked, "Why, with all the bankers hereabouts, along with distinguished councilmen, state legislators, a few men with bridges named after them, did you choose Ryan as our man?"

"Wendell? Five percent. Prime rate. Most folks were a point higher. Wendell's own bank is a point over. His bank is above prime, but he likes to think of himself as gettin' in on the ground floor. Besides, he's on a first-name basis with a TV star, Boy. Save your classy bankers for loans we can pay back."

As Bill got behind the wheel, Casey Lee yanked off his black string tie and loosened the top button on his starched white shirt. Bill hadn't noticed before, but it was clear he had gotten dressed up for the banker. Ryan wouldn't recognize him on the street in five minutes, but Casey Lee probably knew it.

"Been a lot of booms and busts in Florida, but the boom this time looks like a smasher, Bull. Wendell Ryan will come to hate that number five. Before he does, he'll come to know the two of us real good. This ride up could be the living end if we hustle. We'll stick that five percent right up his…Wendell."

Casey Lee pointed down the road, and Bill drove away. They didn't say another word all the way to the office.

Crackers, Bill thought.

Everything that happened at the bank went the way Casey Lee said. Bill kept expecting him to give his opinion on the envelope of receipts and the ramifications.

As they arrived at the office, Bill asked, "Casey Lee, you'd agree, wouldn't you, that we seem to be in a certain amount of danger?"

"Uh-huh."

"Those receipts were in a Rolling R envelope and stashed in a desk in a double-wide that once belonged to Tray Robertson?"

"That I know."

"Well," he said, exasperated, "what do you think we should do?"

Casey Lee stared out the windshield as if squinting at the late-morning sun. In a guttural whisper, he said, "We stand back-to-back in a silence you have yet to learn, and we sleep in shifts in the groves and thickets, if that must be, until they come." He turned quickly away, facing out the passenger window.

Bill expected him to turn back wearing his subtle Christy grin or at least a smirk. When he turned, though, Bill saw a face that was indescribably complex in its range of emotions, but in that instant, Bill saw the face of pure animal rage—his skin was red with expanded temple vessels, his eyes were bloodshot and blazing like torches, while tears glistened on his cheeks like silver war paint.

"Then I will take their lives that they cannot take ours," Casey Lee said softly. "This I swear to you."

It sounded like he was reiterating the law.

CHAPTER NINE
DON'T COUNT GIVING MY BODY IN RETURN

The sun burned through Bill's closed eyelids, turning his vision orange and translucent. Bill pressed his back against the hot sand, working his butt back and forth until the sand filled the contours. His mouth ballooned, as he exhaled and relaxed. It was the best physical therapy since he'd arrived in Florida, but it was only physical.

Bogged down mentally, he was caught up in the threat hanging over him and Casey Lee. He felt haunted by fear, not to mention pain, as he lay in the hospital after his body hit the asphalt, but the current situation was different. He felt he was going to die, not by accident, disease, or an unknown cause, but by an unknown hand at an unknown time and place. He felt like he was being stalked.

At night, he stared through his closed eyelids, unable to sleep, while questions tumbled through his mind constantly. They closed in every time he tried to relax, day or night, even at the present moment on the beach.

Mickey chose the beach, saying it was certain to be deserted. "I promise this will be God's real Florida."

She was right.

They were a mile or more north of John's Island, a very exclusive residential community.

"That's where you'll live someday," she announced when they arrived and stepped onto the warm sand. She turned her face to the shore breeze, drew in salt air, and rushed to the water. The breaking wavelets were small, barely able to crawl up the beach. Strings of disappearing diamonds washed over her feet. She danced in the freshets like a ballerina, a nearly nude one in her tiny black bikini. The two of them could have been naked. There wasn't a soul in either direction on the beach.

The September day felt warm, though it was stifling for anyone inland. On the beach, a gentle, cool, southeasterly fanned across the beach, rolled over the two of them, and combed the dunes behind them, making the dune grass whisper.

He almost slept, the orange behind his eyelids faded, but the questions and fears clicked repetitively through his mind, never quite allowing sleep.

Casey Lee's analysis hadn't helped. "Whoever's trying to zap you wants to get rid of me, too. They bungled it once and stowed those receipts to make me look guilty. Had you died like you were supposed to, they'd have dropped those receipts in the mail to the cops. Better yet, they could send them to your daddy. I'd be indicted for murder.

"Someone blew the job, but who...and why? One way or another, they want us both taken out, so what do we have in common? It's Burton Groves, Incorporated. Somebody wants us off that land, Boss, bad enough to kill. What's worse, if you remember the saying, if at first you don't succeed..."

Bill's eyes popped open from his semidream state, and he blurted, "Try, try again!"

The voice that answered him wasn't Casey Lee. It was demure, sexy, feminine, and whispery.

"Shall we try it now?" Mickey asked.

He realized she dropped down to straddle him dripping wet. "Come on, Lover. I'm sorry. I was just kidding." Her voice trailed off. "I scared you."

Her knees, locked against his ribs, relaxed, and she daubed his sweaty forehead with a towel, hunching over him. "What is it, Poor Baby?"

He wiped a forearm over his face, trying to blink away his thoughts. "I guess I was in the clouds."

"More like a nightmare, if you ask me. What does that mean, 'try, try again.'"

"Let's forget it."

She pulled away.

"Casey Lee thinks they'll try again."

"Who?"

"We don't know, Mickey. We don't know anything."

"Of course not." Her tone suggested shutting her out would hurt her feelings. She eased onto her back beside him, barely touching.

"Somebody's giving Casey Lee and me a hard time."

"Ah. Casey Lee…Christy, you said? You mentioned him in the car on the way up here. I'm in love with him without meeting him for telling you to take a day off like this."

She was every bit the knockout she was in Palm Beach, maybe more so. She was even sexier. She had a nice tan except where her ample, white, glistening breasts erupted out of the skimpy black bikini. She appeared softer, more natural after their first date, not that she'd been hard or brash that night. She returned the $500 paid her for the Breakers stay plus there was the wonderful rose. She asked him to call and he finally did. He told himself he was just being polite. He paid only for dinner and drinks, nothing more. All true.

This was their second date since the Breakers. She suggested a day in the sun, and there hadn't been a word about payment.

"At the risk of prodding, have you talked to Tray Robertson?" she asked. "He might be able to tell you something. Hell, he could probably help."

"No."

"I would."

"Mickey, he's a big man around here, for Christ's sake. I didn't know that when we met at the airport, but he's a politician. People say he might be governor. He's bound to know some weirdoes, but that doesn't mean he knows people who…"

"He knows some real beauties in Palm Beach," she said. "I can tell you that." She rose up to lean on one arm. "When he arranged our date, he didn't call himself. No, an associate called, a guy who sounded like he came from one of the Islands, with the biggest goddamn Brit accent you ever heard. Could there possibly be a Bahamian reggae singer with a British accent?"

He didn't even chuckle. She studied his face, his eyes closed again.

"Up here, he's a king, Mickey," Bill said. "Everybody likes and respects him."

"Yeah."

Bill opened his eyes. "I'm scared, Mickey. I admit it."

"Where's Tray Robertson?"

He shrugged.

"I'm sure his father would know."

*　*　*

The ad in the weekly promised, *Walk to the beach.* The mom-and-pop owners and managers of Beach Efficiencies, Bea and Charles Schneider, were delighted to have a young man move in. They were thrilled when he said he'd be there a minimum of ninety days.

Bea offered him the off-season rate and promptly showed him Unit 2, adjoining theirs, Unit 1. Units 3 and 4, the only others, were empty.

Charles frowned. "The boy might like some privacy."

Bea glared at him, but neither wanted to lose their customer. Gone were the days when mom-and-pop efficiencies were preferred and often the only choice. They weren't full until March or April anymore, not until the new hotels and motels were booked.

"Delighted to have the company," Charles said. "It's a little slow what with hurricane season."

"What with it being off season and all," Bea corrected. "Besides, you haven't recited the Rules and Restrictions. He's obviously single, and there might be stray women coming in and out."

Charles shushed her but agreed to put Mr. Burton in Unit 2.

★   ★   ★

Standing in his new efficiency living area, barefoot and shirtless in Bermuda shorts, Bill asked, "What are you doing now?"

After spending a glorious September Saturday on the beach, then dinner, it grew late, and she stayed over. When Sunday morning arrived, Mickey still hadn't indicated any desire to leave.

The embarrassing question came to him, *is it all costing me money?* Most of the weekend, he hadn't even considered the subject.

She didn't seem like a hooker. She was a total doll, not the right type, without a rough edge anywhere on her. Even her hooker getup for the night at the Breakers hadn't seemed real. It was more like a charade or an act. She was aggressive, yes, but not tough.

Shouldn't she at least chew gum? he wondered.

She sat cross-legged on the floor, in white shorts and bikini bra. She uncrossed her legs and tucked them under her to study a huge paper chart she unfolded on the coffee table.

Sensing him standing there, she replied, "What am I doing? I'm plotting a course."

She took out silver navigator's dividers from a leather Weems and Plath kit and walked the points east along a brass parallel rule laid out along a fine pencil line that ran east and west, from Lake Worth Inlet at Palm Beach to north of West End, Grand Bahamas.

Bill leaned over her shoulder to read the label on the big chart. *Florida East Coast, Gulf Stream, and Northern Bahama.*

"Are those your navigational instruments?" he asked.

"Uh-huh."

"Your chart?"

"No." She drew a straight line running north and south across the inlet's mouth. "It's off the boat."

"The boat?"

"Uh-huh. Watch." She marched the dividers up the north-south line two-and-a-half nautical miles north of Palm Beach and put a dot on the line. "You can't get from here to West End, Grand Bahamas, by sailing west to east. This line I drew is the desired true course, called the *rhumb line.* You get set north about two-and-a-half nautical miles an hour by the current from the Gulf Stream."

He decided it was a game.

She added, "Mariners think of the Gulf Stream as a forty-five-mile-wide river flowing north in the Atlantic Ocean."

At the top of the north line, at the dot she made, she reached with her dividers and opened them to fifteen nautical miles, then put a dot on the rhumb line where the dividers intersected. "*Voilà!* I draw a vector..."

She connected the two dots with a straight line using the parallel rule. That line ran northwest to southeast.

"...like so. The vector is the heading, or the actual direction you have to sail to compensate for the set, which is..." She walked the vector, using her parallel rule to the nearest compass rose and noted the exact magnetic degree shown on the rose. "...110 degrees."

She felt his eyes on her shoulder, absolutely incredulous. She knew if she stopped talking, she'd lose him.

"Now..." She opened the dividers and measured from the mouth of the Inlet at Palm Beach to where the vector intersected the rhumb line. "This is the speed over the bottom in one hour. See? It's slower than the boat speed. It's fifteen knots, so the journey takes longer than you might think if you simply divide the distance by the boat speed. That's where most amateurs make their mistake and wonder why there's still ocean out front as far as the eye can see when they use faulty calculations. They think they should be at West End, Grand Bahamas."

She glanced over her shoulder at him. "Of course, you know all this, being a hotshot sailboat racer on Long Island Sound, right?"

She casually erased the unnecessary and imaginary pencil marks from the chart. The silence that followed seemed eternal.

"Did those races take up your entire Saturday morning?" she asked. "Surely not. That would mean missing your tennis lesson at the Club, wouldn't it? Hmmm? Can I get you a beer?"

She walked across the room to the kitchenette and reached into the refrigerator.

Without moving a muscle, he followed her with his eyes. "Mickey, about three vectors back, I asked you a question."

"They're ice cold. I brought chips just for you, Captain Bull. Oh, I like that. Aye, aye, Captain Bull. Ready about! Hard-a-lee!"

"Mickey?" He started to get up.

"OK, OK." She trudged back to the coffee table with two ice-cold green bottles in one hand and a bag of chips in the other, and plopped down. "Then you be first mate, and I'll be captain." She smiled.

"Mickey?"

"I am one, you know—U.S. Coast Guard licensed captain, charter boats, six passengers or less."

"Are you going to tell me what's going on?"

"Plus I spent summers on a Bahamas charter boat out of Fort Lauderdale...mating."

"Mating?"

"First mating, to you. Oh, all right. I'll tell you. It belongs to a friend. It's a thirty-five-foot Bertram Sports fisherman, with radar, GPS, and everything. I chartered it."

"You chartered a boat?"

"I'm going to the Bahamas."

"I see. You mean you're being taken by one of...your clients."

"It's my charter. I'm going alone, except, possibly with one or two crew. Think I'll have any trouble getting crew, Bill?"

"Why, for God's sake?"

"Your situation up there interests me."

"What do you mean? What's this have to do with a vacation?"

"Trent Robertson sounded positively sexy on the phone when I called. He was pleased to pass on the message that one of Tray's many female admirers called. He said Tray's in the Bahamas Bill."

"Mickey, what's with Tray Robertson? Yesterday, you suggested he might not be able to help."

"I'm not talking about your getting a hard time from a bunch of redneck assholes, and I didn't necessarily mean that Robertson would help voluntarily."

"I'm lost. I don't understand how any of this is a concern of yours."

"Come here." She pulled Bill to sit cross-legged in front of her, waiting for his eyes to lock onto hers. "I first saw Tray Robertson in Palm Beach at all the better spots. I was attracted, I admit. He's a big-deal rancher. I thought maybe I'd found my Marlboro Man, but a couple of girls I know went out with him. Tray isn't very nice to women, Bill."

His jaw almost dropped open, but she pushed it shut with one hand. "Shush. Anyway, he started calling me. He became aggressive and started hounding me, so I put out word with some of the lowlifes around here that I was a pro."

He backed away in surprise.

"I kept up the hoax," she continued. "It became my..."

"You're telling me you aren't?"

"Not unless you count giving my body to a guy in return for skydiving lessons."

He studied her face for several seconds, then he smiled in relief. He'd been right all along. She wasn't a hooker.

He suddenly became serious again. "I think you let this become an obsession. Going to the Bahamas? Following people?"

"Bill, let me tell you something. My parents, the Morgan-Lloyds, are wealthy people on Palm Beach. All my life, they've been what's called casual or social opioid users. They're addicts. They use oxycodone, cocaine, and fentanyl with heroin—a major cause of overdoses.

"I started as a teenager and became highly self-trained in illegal substances, addiction, treatment, and trafficking. I didn't have much choice. Every day, ninety Americans die from overdosing. I tried everything with them. They have the money, so their sources never dry up. It comes in from Miami, through Central America via China.

"When they go out for the evening, people say they're distraught over their daughter's chosen profession, which my parents let leak on purpose. They're distraught, all right, but it isn't because I'm supposedly a hooker. It's because they're afraid I'll get them busted."

He mulled that over for a moment. "Knowing all this makes you have to follow Tray Robertson through the Bahamas?"

Mickey, leaning back, braced herself on locked arms. Her head cocked, as she smiled at him for thinking she was crazy. "Bill, I'm trying to add one and one and get two."

They argued for hours.

She said she chartered the boat for only a few days, so she could run over to the Islands and have a look around. He insisted the idea was ridiculous that Tray was likely skippering a yacht for a wealthy family.

"I'm going with or without you," she said.

"I don't know anything about running around in the Bahamas in a boat."

"I do. I've done it dozens of times. You've been a sailor. You must have some power-boat experience."

"Well, yes. My father owns offshore fishing boats. We've taken trips to Block Island Sound, Martha's Vineyard, and Nantucket. I can handle a boat, but if I had even the slightest connection between Tray and anything illegal, I'd hand it over to the authorities and let them handle it."

He stood and walked to the window, staring out at the purple bougainvillea across the street.

"The authorities don't give a damn about you," she said softly. "If there's a big opioid ring involved, they'll peg the top dogs before they move in. Believe me, you'd be dead by then. Do you want that? Do you want this to go on as it is?"

Dear God, no, he thought, slowly shaking his head.

"The U.S. government doesn't want it to go on, either."

Exasperated, he asked, "How the hell would you know, Mickey?"

"Maybe I'm just a smart girl, Bill." She sighed. "It's late. I've got a headache."

"I didn't know people still got headaches."

"Some people give me headaches." She turned her head slowly on her long, thin neck, black hair sweeping her face, and decided to gamble. She kept it up, adding some sexy sighs and moans.

"Is there anything I can do?" he asked.

★　　★　　★

On the front of Unit 1 at Beach Efficiencies, Bea and Charles Schneider rocked gently on their hanging swing. They did that almost every evening until eight-thirty or nine o'clock, listening to the ocean thump and crunch on the beach 500 yards away, just beyond the condos and beach resorts.

Long after midnight, Charles took in the cool night air and exhaled loudly, his lips fluttering in the silence. "Sounds like it's all quiet next door."

"I'd almost forgotten how beautiful the nights can be. Remember spending those all-nighters on the beach?"

He remembered, wondering if it was the cool night air that brought on Bea's rare reverie. "I'll move him down to Unit 4 tomorrow."

"We'd eat and drink and go skinny-dipping all hours. The beach belonged to us. Remember?"

"You gonna sit out here till dawn, Bea?"

"Charlie?"

CHAPTER TEN
GULF STREAM CROSSING: ON THE SERPENT'S BACK

The Bertram ripped and snorted eastward at eighteen knots on an uneven ocean. Below, over the noise and hull vibration, the marine radio speaker crackled, then blared:

"This... United Stat... Weather Bureau Radio, broad... on VHF 24 hours a... on 162.4 Megahertz. Follow... special... Advisory #2... 10 A.M. EST September 29. Tropical Storm Camellia is upgraded...hurricane strength. Hurricane warnings...windward and leeward... including Virgin Islands and... Hurricane watch... affect Dominican Rep... Haiti, the Bahamas, and Southeast Florida. All parties... following areas... stand by... further... prepared to..."

Mickey, lunging across the main saloon, slapped the VHF receiver to Off, hoping the VHF on the bridge couldn't be heard or wasn't monitoring the weather channel. If Bill heard, he'd insist they turn back.

She waited, hearing nothing from on top, no stomping on the cabin sole. The intercom between galley and bridge didn't bellow. There was only the phlegmy, high-speed moan of the two bronze propellers churning below.

She decided to go up. A cold beer and plastic cup in each hand, she popped the hook on the aft door and started up the ladder. It was difficult enough with both hands full, the boat unquestionably rolling more. She felt the hull buck in the increasingly strong current. As she moved up the rungs, shocks of wind grabbed at her.

Slipping behind the helmsman's seat, she leaned against the aft rail with her legs apart. Her tan thighs contrasted brightly with her short, white cut-offs. She wore a flaming-pink T-shirt and matching baseball cap, which was placed on her head backward against the wind.

"We're on the apex of the Gulf Stream, Captain," she shouted, reaching over his shoulder with the beer and cup while looking around. "In the center of the Stream, the current's faster, four to six-knot drift. We're going north as fast as we're going east, Captain."

"Yeah. I can sense it." He remembered Mickey's lecture on the Gulf Stream set and felt the starboard engine groan with the additional torque. The wake, snow white against the infamous dark, ink-blue water of the Stream, churned north, as the boat plowed east.

The earlier gentle rollers, which came closer together, were now four-foot waves with momentum built in. Their new muscle slugged at the hull, causing ripping and roaring sounds, as shafts of air tried to break the plane. The thirty-five-foot Bertram was starboard side-to on the serpent's back, riding the rapids of the great Atlantic River.

Bill, crossing the Gulf Stream for the first time, never felt anything like it before. He scanned the horizon for other life, but there was nothing as far as he could see. It was a beautiful day with clear-blue sky. Big cumulus cloud formations floated off the starboard bow over Northwest Providence Channel on the south side of Grand Bahama.

Mickey suggested the clouds were a good way to spot Grand Bahama in the afternoon. She told him , "Look for big boomers gathering over the island's south shore."

She watched the skipper lean to port. With his back to her, Mickey slipped closer to the stainless-steel wheel and helmsman's console, checking the VHF radio and LORAN. The radio was set to channel 16, the Call/Distress channel, so Bill couldn't have heard the weather. The LORAN screen printed navigational information on Waypoint One, their first landfall.

You are 7NM south of course.
You are 37NM from WYPT.

"Thirty-seven miles to go," she said.

"How come we're off course, Navigator?"

"Loran doesn't know about the set, Captain. We're getting carried on course. You'll see." Mickey relished any opportunity to flirt and tease her crewmate. "We'll be pretty much on target by the time we clear the Stream." She faciously batted black eyelashes at him.

By four o'clock that afternoon, the sun turned the rocky shoreline of Waypoint One, West End Point, Grand Bahama Island, a hundred shades of copper. Lines of *casuarinas* trees on the shore had silver highlights.

The Little Bahama Bank beyond West End Point fanned out its turquoise waters for 3,000 square miles to the east. Miles out on the Bank, a dozen yachts and Bahamian commercial fishing boats gleamed chalk-white in the late sun. A few in the distance, poised on the sharp edge of the horizon, appeared lifted on pedestals.

A mile offshore, west of the harbor, they throttled down to Slow/Forward. Three sticks in the water marked the dogleg channel that skirted the canyon wall on the edge of the Bahama Bank. Fierce tidal currents poured off and on the Bank most of the time, and water depth went from sixty fathoms to one in less than a boat length. Beyond the channel was the inner harbor and West End, Grand Bahama's Jack Tar Hotel.

The skipper stopped the boat. Mickey came onto the fishing deck dressed in a khaki wraparound skirt with cute, offset pelican needlepoint on it, and a white cotton Polo shirt with the collar open and up. She looked to the bridge, one hand shielding her eyes with a comb in the other.

"I think we should have a plan," Bill shouted.

Mickey, with her "captain's ticket" and experience, would skipper the Bertram in. On her charter jobs, the boats left from here, and she was familiar with the harbor. She planned to radio the dockmaster for a slip and check in with customs.

Mainly, they planned to scour the docks for familiar faces and the "big Burger," following Trent Robertson's description of the boat Tray would be on. If they saw anyone familiar, they planned to leave.

"Let's not ask questions about this even of the dockmaster and the Customs people," Mickey said. "Not that everyone is corrupt, but we can't assume anything. Asking the wrong person could be fatal." She thought for a second. "Or so I'm told.

"Among the young Bahamian boys are small-time thieves, dope peddlers, runners, and lookouts. They occupy the lowest chain of command that runs all the way to Nassau, Miami, and even New York.

"We're tourists, so we should act like tourists. You'll see some low-level bosses hanging around the hotel lobby and the bar, the Sit and Be Damned."

"The sit and be what?"

"Damned. The Sit and Be Damned is the hotel bar. The hotel gets a lot of single amateur ladies, in twos and fours and groups, along with lots of Canadians, fly-in tours, two- or three-day packages sold cheap. They don't see much except the Sit and Be Damned."

* * *

Docking went well. They didn't see any big yachts. The harbor was two-thirds full with thirty- to forty-footers, including a number of high-performance cruisers, which might have been promising, but they all had families aboard. There were half a dozen fishing boats, their extensive tackle suggesting serious fishing and nothing more, with the same number of cruising sailboats.

Mickey backed the boat into their assigned slip, they tied up, and they walked around the dock to the dockmaster's shed. As they entered, Bill pointed at the men's room door adjacent to the office, while Mickey went into the office.

"Well, Mates, you must be 180 off course, but aren't we all?" asked the crisp Aussie dockmaster.

"What's the latest on the hurricane?" Mickey asked.

"Not much change, Missy. She's a few days away yet."

The dockmaster assigned them a very nice slip, stern-to against the outer west wall. Their evening view over the transom would be a tepid, moonlit Bahama Bank—very romantic. Forward from the bridge, they'd be able to see anyone coming down the docks from the hotel.

Bahamian Customs and Immigration personnel passed them through with barely a pause, which was Mickey's doing, of course. It was also "after five," and the officers chattered to each other. They still had a five-thirty Canadian package flight to clear.

* * *

Bill showered, shaved, and dressed. Mickey made drinks. He emerged from the cabin in khakis and a blue button-down shirt, carrying a blue blazer and striped tie loose around his neck, and joined Mickey on the aft deck to enjoy the Bahama Bank at evening.

He started to ask if he needed a coat and tie, but she put her fingers to her lips, and they listened to the harbor.

The peppery fume of salt and exposed sea growth cleared their sinuses. Barnacles clicked and snapped, gasping on exposed bulkheads. Water gurgled around pilings and snaked out the harbor entrance. The tide slipped off the Little Bahama Bank in countless spokes from ever-changing centers like water running off a platter.

They had one last drink, then they stepped off the boat and walked to the asphalt lane that curved toward the hotel.

"You caused me a problem in the men's room."

"Oh?"

"The dockmaster's shed has thin walls. I peed on myself about the hurricane."

"I'm sorry. I was waiting for a good time to tell you."

"Like at dinner? I'm glad I had to go when I did. What do you think?"

"It's only a hurricane *watch*, Bill. It's a long way off, and we're here." Taking his hand, she pulled him off the blacktop toward the near end of the sprawling hotel.

They walked through the double doors and down the long hall with numbered doors on either side.

"I learned this shortcut when it was pouring rain one day," Mickey explained. "We can slip into the main lobby from the side, rather than plunge through the main entrance. The lobby is huge and usually crowded."

The Jack Tar's Grand Lobby, approximately 100 feet square, had fifty-foot ceilings, with gold marble walls rising halfway on all sides, and gold paint sheathed the high ceilings. As Mickey said, the lobby was huge, bright, and loud.

Under a twenty-foot-wide winding stairway to the dining room was the Sit and Be Damned. Opposite was the entrance, where a gang of double French doors ran the length of the lobby.

The young Black male population of West End was gathered by the front doors, pushing shoving, laughing, and showing off for each other. The younger ones tried to impress the ones in the tailored Edwardian suits.

Suddenly, for a second, Bill's eyes connected with a Bahamian kid, who stared back without blinking.

"That kid—don't look—by the doors," Bill said. "We looked at each other. I thought he'd say something."

"You know him?"

"Yes. I know I do, but from where?"

"Let's sit down, shall we?"

They sauntered halfway across the lobby and settled into chairs where they could glance at the kid without appearing to stare.

"Which one is he?" she asked quietly.

He eyed the group, then turned to her and shrugged. "Huh. Don't see him now. Where have I seen him before?"

"He'll show. He can't go far. He's probably never been off the island."

He looked at her. "Yes, he has. I just don't know where."

She didn't want to make a big deal of a gawking boy, who was hardly the prey they wanted. "It'll come to you." She glanced at her watch. "Shall we go up? Our table's ready, I'm sure, and so am I—white linens, fine china, good crystal, and the best Dover sole in the Islands."

Crossing the lobby, Bill scanned various faces, being friendly, going for eye contact, but even the ones who laughed went sullen and dead-eyed when they met his gaze. They didn't say or do anything, just looked through him, not unfriendly but certainly not friendly, either.

The four French-speaking girls ahead of them on the staircase didn't get the same treatment. They all got eye contact and more from the boys in the lobby.

"The five-thirty tour flight from Toronto," Mickey whispered. "Your Canadian girls."

An unamused, stocky, huffing and puffing waiter with a shiny ebony forehead and bulging double-breasted white dinner jacket, whisked the four ladies into the dining room without a flourish, understanding full well they would know only two English words, *Gratuity Included.*

The maître d' stand was left tended by a tall, thin, older, walnut-colored gentleman with short, salt-and-pepper hair, crisp in a black tux. He greeted the couple with warmth and class.

"Good evening. My name is Regis." He gave a slight bow. "Welcome to the Jack Tar."

"Thank you, Regis," Mickey said. "I thought the lobby would follow right on up and join us."

"No, Madame." He held his head high and quietly added, "Not yet. A couple more years, then they'll be up here."

"What do you mean?"

"Independence, Madame. Bahamian independence. We're still adjusting."

Mickey smiled, and he gave her an almost-invisible wink.

"Will the Jack Tar survive it, Regis?"

"No, Madame. Not the Jack Tar we know." He spoke as if the words were rehearsed, his eyes on hers.

Then he looked at Bill and asked for his name without actually saying a word.

"Oh, Schneider. Charles Schneider."

★　★　★

"Kill him."

Tray Robertson shot from his chair and across the main salon of the luxury yacht *Enchantress* before he could stop himself. He clamped his hands on his hips, making the epaulets of his white skipper's shirt loop up, and glared at the docks baking in the dusky sun.

"Mr. Caraja, we have no fucking idea who the man is the kid saw," he said, his back to the others.

The fat little Columbia hood slumped on the L-shaped settee, his mouth open, as if sucking a cigar that wasn't there. A napkin-wrapped rum and Coke sweated in his hand. He was shirtless, and his red Bermuda shorts hung to his knees, belted under his fat gut. Roosevelt Awbrey half-sat on a stool at the bar against the salon's forward bulkhead. His faded orange shirt with white batik palm trees hung loosely over his extra-large faded cut-offs.

Tray annoyed by the man's dull ruthlessness, was determined to keep a lid on the situation.

"We have it that Rosey's kid thought the guy looked familiar. Little Winny got a look when I picked up the man at the stateside airport. That's if the kid was paying attention and can remember every face he sees two months later. Jesus Christ." He tried to calm himself, watching the activity at the dock and beyond at the pool and bar.

They were docked at Conch Inn, the best spot in Marsh Harbour, except for the heat. Marsh Harbour, with its horseshoe shape, was in the lee of the prevailing southeasterly breeze, and Conch Inn lay tucked in at the crotch.

Aboard the Burger, Hector Caraja sweated, though the yacht's massive air-conditioning worked night and day.

"Quite true," Rosey said sleepily, "and Tray has a good point, Mr. No Wet. I checked the hotel, and the guy wasn't registered, and not at the marina, either. I called the dining room myself. The maître d' said no names starting with B had reservations last night."

Hector looked from one man to the other, nodded, and puckered his lips like a Butterfly fish, as if considering their advice. Then he said flatly and evenly, "Find him, then kill him."

Tray threw up his hands and stormed forward, shaking his head, as he passed Rosey. He disappeared into the pilothouse and up the stairs to the bridge.

When the stomping overhead stopped, and Country Western music blared on the bridge stereo, Hector asked, "Rosey, I ever let you down? When's the last time you had to take some sucker out diving for a few bucks? Am I stupid or new to the racket? Did I run fucking four mil recently through Burton's fucking barn and out through the fucking loft, then dump it on Avenue D in beautiful downtown Fort Pierce fucking Florida? Was that to the tune of fifteen mil? Didn't you find a warm bed for all that money?

"What did our captain do? He takes a fucking trip to Connecticut on his own to run a cockamamie scheme and check out the owner's kid. Did I order that? No. We want that kid to stay home, jack off, fuck Darien's entire female population, go to college, and keep his ass out of the groves. Our captain said he could zap him?

"He put the Cracker kid in to run the groves, because he'll do what he's told, quote unquote. Shit. The kid's like a fucking guard dog. Next? I'm outta here in fourteen hours. Robertson's still there for days. The plane's still there for days, which we damned near lost, 'cause he's gotta police the area for three or four days. Then a week later, it's finally outta there. What's he supposed to be doing for us? Smooth the way for the locals, keep everybody calm, and keep the heat off, right? Shit! We look like shit in Miami in some circles."

Rosey got off the barstool, thinking the man would never quit. He walked aft to look out over the expanse of Marsh Harbour's commercial activity. His boss was within reaching distance, but at least he didn't have to look at the fat white bastard. Two hundred yards astern, six kids splashed each other in the water off the end of the Government Yacht Pier. Beyond them, a small fly bridge sport-fishing rig, probably a Bertram, inched into the big stone Customs Dock. He'd give anything to take someone diving at that moment, even free. He knew what was coming.

Nobody on the floor of the Paris Bourse tutored him for that. When he made deposits in French and German and British banking houses, the officers and partners treated him like royalty, not scum.

"The boys in Miami asked how well we knew our captain, which means, do we know what the fuck we're doing up here? Mostly, it means he hasn't passed the test. They won't let him be a friend, you know?" He sounded almost sympathetic.

Rosey kept staring aft, knowing the words were only seconds away.

"Look, Rosey, after you and the captain get rid of the Citrus King, you get rid of the captain, too."

Rosey winced inside all the way down to his legs. He squeezed his eyes shut harder, keeping them closed. It was as if he could see for eighty-five miles, all the way back to Walker's Cay and up the hill to the club, the pool, and the cabana table with the envelope on it.

He felt something tug on his mind, pulling on him. He was no longer on the yacht, and it wasn't the present moment anymore.

Mama Awbrey's bellowing voice, which could carry across the Bight of Abaco, thundered through his mind. *Remember, Roosevelt T. Awbrey, from whence you come!*

★ ★ ★

Rosey came from a family of divers.

As if he were half-dolphin, he rolled on the surface and dove through the luminous, aquamarine water, down shafts of sunlight dusty with microscopic life, down the tiny strands of bubbles escaping his lips and the watery troughs sliding off his slender black back that looked slate-gray, until he went six fathoms, seven, then eight. Near the bottom, his inflated chest felt but didn't brush the white sand bottom. He glided, losing momentum, becoming motionless, suspended, and hung there as curious as a young barracuda in the slack tide.

He lay one inch off the bottom of a mesa on the leeward side of Mantanilla Shoal, a huge coral formation on the Little Bahama Bank, the northernmost part of the Bahamas Archipelago. It was twenty-five miles from home in Grand Cay, a settlement of Blacks who worked at Walker's Cay Club, the classy sport fishing and hotel complex on neighboring

Walker's Cay. At seventeen, he was in his third year as a professional Bahamian dive guide.

The islands of the area, with little elevation and no rivers, produced no runoff. Four times a day, the Eastern Atlantic tides cleansed it for good measure. Visibility was seventy meters, the clearest water in the world.

The boy knew what he was doing, what he saw, and the environment in which he lay. The giant, billowing black coral heads in front of him were topped with jeweled orange, purple, and yellow stag horn and brain coral and swaying sea fans. Below, in the shadows under overhanging ledges, caves tunneled into undulating blackness. His eyes scanned the upper edges of the caves for the telltale probing of antennae. It took patience at that point in a free dive, willing himself to wait, sacrificing a few more tiny bubbles from his lips. Patience was the hardest part he had to learn, but it made his father famous, and the boy learned well.

Young Roosevelt T. Awbrey hadn't known where the middle initial came from. His mother told him the truth, but he assumed it was a joke, because Mama and Papa joked a lot.

"Dat T stand for Teach, Master William Teach," she said. "You know— the Pirate Blackbeard. You end up just like him, you not listen to your mama."

It could be true, though. She also said Big Papa's ancestors came from Africa first, then Carolina, then down the islands working for privateers, then free boys, finally to the Bahamas. Mama and Big Papa laughed with their heads thrown back when they said certain things. Little Rosey, when he decided they were just having fun and there was nothing to get serious about, laughed like crazy, too. Life was great for him when he was a boy.

Mama ran the show on Grand Cay politically, governmentally, and socially. Mama knew best and called all the shots. Every Grand Cay citizen who climbed aboard a boat was employed at the Walker's Cay Club. They piled onto the Club's water taxis every morning and rode home at night. No worker stayed the night on Walker's Cay. Mama, the workers' representative, knew the work was subsistence, but it was better than the periodic starvation of the past, when the fish house was empty and smelled of rot. Occasionally, a gifted child was sent to Nassau to school, and he never returned. Mama encouraged young people to leave, get good jobs somewhere, send money, and come back only to visit.

Roosevelt Awbrey thought he'd always like life on Grand Cay just fine.

★   ★   ★

Still aft in the *Enchantress'* main salon, gazing out over the harbor without seeing it, he felt several hard tugs, and his gaze jerked back to the moment. Mr. No Wet, still slouched in his chair, had a fistful of the big Bahamian's shirt and pulled on it playfully.

He smiled up at Rosey with drunk eyes and asked, "You know what I mean, Rosey?"

CHAPTER ELEVEN
GET DAT DEMON, OR DAT DEMON GET YOU

The Bertram picked its way onto the Bahama Bank over a brownish bottom and through crystal-clear water that looked shallower than it was. Ahead, the water turned emerald as it went deeper. The thirty-five-footer swung southeasterly, down the Abacos to Marsh Harbour on Great Abaco Island.

Mickey and Bill, on the bridge, felt the breeze in silence.

She said, "Strange scene back there, Captain."

They both tried to understand what happened at West End. First, the Australian dockmaster and his thin, middle-aged Bahamian so-called dock boy exchanged roles.

They checked out at the office first thing in the morning. The dockmaster seemed to be in pain, but it was actually terror or panic in his eyes. Those same eyes had been warm the previous day.

Walking to the boat, they were followed by the dock boy. Nonstop, he wailed some strange island voodoo song, shrieked and gyrated, dancing dangerously close to the bulkhead. The previous day, the boy was speechless and withdrawn all day.

Finally, Bill grabbed the glassy-eyed fool by the shoulder and barked, "That's enough!" He stuffed a twenty in the kid's dirty shirt pocket. "Here. Now git."

The boy, his face almost against Bill's, sang the lyrics of his song with agitated clarity.

Big storm, bad storm;
Get dat demon

Or dat demon

Get you.

Shaking Bill's hand, he transferred a small envelope to him. Suddenly acting cold sober, the boy said, "Receipt for dock. Do not open here."

Shocked, Bill slipped the envelope into his pocket.

A few minutes later, when they were underway and clear of West End, Bill pulled out the receipt and found a note with it.

Lobby boys check on you last night. Knew your name. Thought you should know. Told them nothing.

Regis

Mickey read it and said, "Guess you were right about the kid in the hotel. Jesus. That lunatic dock boy could end up in a chum bucket for delivering this."

"So could Regis for writing it."

"I'm glad we left. We're better off. Marsh Harbour's protected with creeks, hurricane holes, and plenty of charter flights."

He rolled his eyes at the thought of trying to escape at the last minute on a flight. Oddly, the weather overhead at the moment was beautiful.

*   *   *

Seven hours out, at five o'clock in the afternoon, they were a mile off Marsh Harbour, which Trent suggested was a good place to find Tray.

Mickey scanned with binoculars. There was no haze, and the markers for the harbor entrance were visible off the port bow. The day was flawlessly, ominously, clear. The high-pressure air north of the approaching cyclonic mass had been sucked clean of moisture and pollutants.

Mickey stared down the center of the harbor. The sun made the transoms on the big yachts shimmer and pop in blinding whites.

"All the biggies are at the Conch Inn. Hard to tell details." She handed him the glasses.

He adjusted and scanned the north shore, seeing several big homes and a charter outfit. Back down the center were commercial buildings, a fish house, a boatyard, and storage tanks. On the south shore, the Conch Inn sprawled for several hundred yards, a mishmash of stucco and frame buildings, hotel, restaurant, several bars, a boutique, and a pool, all painted soft gray with bright yellow trim.

The Conch Inn offered the biggest, most-elaborate yacht slips in the harbor, complete with electricity and running fresh water, all at a hefty price per foot per day. There wasn't a single empty slip, as if the law prohibited hurricanes, or, as Bill guessed, what was prohibited was undue excitement over *manana*.

Along the southern shore, he studied over their starboard bow a stone and concrete dock, sixty to seventy-five feet in diameter. A small A-frame building stood at the end of the dock, painted khaki green with beige trim. On a yardarm out front, a flag stood smartly in the fresh breeze, the Union Jack in the upper canton and a red field with the Commonwealth of the Bahamas Coat of Arms.

"Customs dock," he said. "There's an officer standing in the doorway. Let's stop and talk to him, maybe take a look around."

"You're the captain." She started down from the bridge.

"Maybe he'll let us stay a minute or two. I'd like to take a quick peak ashore without announcing ourselves to the whole harbor."

Mickey, busy putting out fenders and lines, didn't answer.

Bill brought the Bertram up against the stone dock so it was between them and the rest of the harbor. Big iron cleats on the dock every twenty feet suggested it was used for island freighters.

Mickey stood on the port aft gunwale to throw a line around a dock cleat. A smiling black face leaned over the dock, gave her a snappy nod and smile, then took the line to lace it over the cleat in a flash before the man stood. He wore a crisp white shirt with epaulets, a black tie, and pressed gray shorts.

Bill leaned over the bridge to talk to the young officer, who spoke first.

"You have no quarantine flag, Captain," he stated.

"We've cleared. We're all set, thank you." He started down the bridge ladder and stopped halfway. "We cleared at West End. I hoped you could help us. We're looking for a friend, a Mr. Robertson."

Mickey, stepping off the boat, came up behind Bill.

"May I see your Cruising Permit, please, Captain?"

Mickey held out the permit, and the officer accepted it with a grin. "I don't believe I know a Mr. Robertson. What's he look like?"

"Captain Tray," Mickey said. "We're looking for Captain Tray."

The Bahamian smiled broadly. "Oh, Captain Tray. Of course, Mon. Everybody know Captain Tray. Conch Inn, out at end of dock, big motor yacht. You see." He pointed. "Name is *Enchantress.* Very nice. You see now?"

Bill saw the name on the beamy transom. It was a beautiful luxury yacht, at least seventy feet long.

"Got it. One more thing." Bill shook the officer's hand and crunched a twenty against the man's palm. "I wonder if we could leave the boat for a bit, run up to make a phone call?"

"I can allow that, yes."

"Mickey, you want to hold down the ship just in case?" He gave her a quick wink.

"Sure." She gave the young officer a look and wink that almost buckled his knees. "We'll keep an eye on things, won't we, Officer? What was your name?"

"Matthew, Ma'am."

"Matthew? How about a beer, Officer Matthew?"

Bill, nodding at them, walked down the dock.

The town of Marsh Harbour occupied a few hundred yards in both directions. He stopped and watched a young man leave Barclays Bank. He wore a well-tailored light cord suit, a conservative three piece. His complexion was like milk chocolate, he was rail thin and he looked barely out of his teens except for his receding hair. Although he didn't look like a local, if he was, he might know the wrong people.

Bill decided to take a chance. "Sir? I wonder if you might help me out?"

"If I possibly can, delighted. What can I do for you?" He spoke without a discernible accent.

"I know you're closed, but—this sounds foolish—but some time ago, I rented a safe-deposit box, either here at Barclays or one of the others. There are just three banks, right?"

"Yes, Sir, although we like to think..."

"Could you check for me to see if mine is here?"

"Well, it's a little..."

He smiled at the youngster and held out his hand. "You aren't a local boy, are you?"

"No, Sir. Toronto."

When their hands met, the man added, "How do you do, Sir? My name is Cooper Hanna. I was sent down to, shall we say, assist for a while a couple weeks ago."

"No wonder we haven't met, Cooper. My name is Casey Lee Christy."

Cooper smiled. "Of course, Mr. Christy. Yes. I haven't had the pleasure until now, although I've met a couple of your associates here at the bank."

"Getting things in and out of the box?"

"Yes, Sir, and making deposits and withdrawals from the account."

"Of course." Bill nodded in agreement. "Well, that settles it, then, doesn't it?"

"Sir?"

"My safe deposit box is right here, right where I thought."

"Yes, Sir, it is. Shall we see you tomorrow, then?"

"Fine, Cooper. I look forward to it."

Bill turned away and walked east toward the telephone company and a bank of pay phones. It was after five, and he didn't want to miss Casey Lee.

He was ready to break into a trot when he heard someone calling behind him.

"Mr. Christy! Mr. Christy!"

He almost didn't turn around, then he stopped and turned.

Cooper Hanna had his hands cupped to his mouth and shouted, "Nine A.M. until only one P.M. Bahamian banking hours. Nice, huh? I'll be in Nassau, but anyone can help you. Oh, and best to keep an ear to the radio, what with the weather. See you again."

He should have shouted, "Thank you!" but his mouth was too dry, and nothing came out. Bill waved instead.

He ran to the phone, picked up a receiver, and placed a collect call person-to-person to his partner.

"Hello? Bill?" he asked.

"No, you're Bill. This is Casey Lee, your partner. You OK otherwise? You sound a little out of breath."

"I'm OK. You?"

"We own 1,000 more acres that I could use a little help with. You know anyone who can sit still long enough to get it into production before they foreclose on us?"

"You closed on the new property?"

"Yeah. Couldn't find any so-called management, which made Arthur Wendell Ryan smart a little, but we had to pick the fruit. It was part of the deal, crop on the tree, plus get rolling on planting resets and budlings before next winter's freeze, ya know. When I told Wendell you were blue marlin fishing with some big shot from Palm Beach, shee-it, he damn near dribbled in his pinstripes. Besides, we had Power of Attorney in the company file."

"I don't recall signing any..."

"What's that I'm hearing? Sounds like your plain ol' rude Yankee talk to me, Mista Burton."

"I remember now. Sure. How could I have forgotten?"

"Hey, Boss, is there a reason for this call?"

He leaned against the half-booth cubicle. "I want you to fly here tomorrow first thing, charter something A.M. and get over here. Bring every piece of ID you have."

"What's up?"

"I want you to open your safe deposit box at Barclays Bank for me."

Casey Lee chuckled. "I don't have a..."

"Now, Boy, what's this I'm hearing? Sounds like your typical dumb Cracker talk to me."

"Bull," Casey Lee said, suddenly serious. "Where am I going?"

"Marsh Harbour airport. Take a cab to town to the government yacht pier just west of the Conch Inn. It's a resort, gray with yellow trim. You can't miss it, but don't show your face around there unless you want to run into some people you aren't that close to."

"OK. What about the hurricane?"

"You tell me. I haven't checked in hours." Bill heard Casey Lee shuffling telex reports on his desk. "Let's see. Two hundred miles east of Barbados, turned northwest. That must've been late yesterday. Continuing at plus-minus twenty knots. Present position, P.M., 19.3 degrees north latitude by 62.2 west longitude. That's about 200 miles east-northeast of the British Virgin Islands. Expected Camellia landfall Northern Bahamas/Florida Southeast coast area twenty-four to thirty-six hours.

"I'd say that Marsh Harbour and our Florida area will go from Hurricane Watch to Warning by about midday tomorrow. If it comes, I really need to be here."

"And do what?"

"Well, nothing."

"OK. Get shakin', Mista Christy. Sounds like we're running out of time."

"Bull, I thought I might bring a friend. You mind?"

"You know someone who wants to go shark hunting in a hurricane?"

"I sure do, and she just happens to know what a certain big, Black Bahamian looks like, which is more than we know."

Bill paused and stared at the receiver in his hand. "Holy shit."

He heard Casey Lee laugh, then hang up.

"'Bye, Casey Lee."

Mickey and Bill moved the boat from Customs to the Yacht pier, cleaned up, showered, and changed. The Marsh Harbour sky over the harbor entrance turned a tangerine color, with shades of pink and shimmering brass. Directly overhead, the air felt thread-thin, a pure frigid blue so crisp and clear it reminded him of the skydiver's sky at 10,000 feet.

They made drinks in the main salon at the bar Mickey stocked, then went on the aft deck. Lights came on aboard the yachts, including the *Enchantress,* which showed every light she had. Yellow power cables hung from her like umbilical cords running to dockside.

She's gonna ride it out here, Bill thought. *She won't give away any secrets, like where they get the stuff, where they load it, and how they do it. I doubt there are large quantities of opioids aboard. Something the size of a seldom-used barn would do just fine, wouldn't it?*

"Well?" Mickey asked.

"Have I thanked you for getting this all together, getting me here, and sticking with me?"

"Not in the last thirty-six hours, but that's all right. I somehow forgot about kissin' and huggin' when murderers are docked next door and will probably occupy the next table at dinner tonight."

"Might well be."

She shrugged. "We can't just sit here and glare at them all week. Let's face it. We have to get involved, hang ourselves out here like..."

"Live bait?"

"Exactly."

"You know something? There are only two people in my world I can't outfox—you and Casey Lee Christy. When he looks at you, you might as well be stark naked."

Feigning a shudder, she said, "I can't wait to meet him and his girlfriend."

"You never know about him. I think she's just a friend. She's the one who knit this whole thing together to some extent. She's even met one of them."

Hearing the stomp of hard heels on the dock, they turned to see Officer Matthew, as he left the dock, stepped onto the portside catwalk, and handed Mickey a piece of notepaper.

"Captain Tray asked me to give you this." He immediately about-faced and stepped back to the dock, walking away quickly.

"Doesn't want to get involved," Mickey said, reading the note.

Come on up for dinner. I'll say hello as if I know you, introduce you around. Maybe we can work something out.
Tray

"What? He's the Conch Inn social director now? Pardon me."
"'Work something out?'" Bill repeated. "About the weather?"
She frowned.
"Well?"
The Conch Inn's famous island ambiance enveloped them, as they walked through the vestibule. A waitress, one of the young Eleutheran girls with demure smiles and eyes that said, *Welcome* as only Eleutherans could say, this one cool and placid, thoroughly composed in her white, lace serving dress, ushered them to a table overlooking the harbor.

The airy dining room's harborside exterior walls were made of tall, white-painted wooden horizontal louvers in frames, open to the outside air and without glass. White ceiling fans turned slowly against the white ceiling. Flower arrangements and tall plants contrasted with the white background. It was ten degrees cooler than outside, without any sound, smell, or indication of air-conditioning.

His dinner date was cool, attractive, and laid back, even under the circumstances. A batik blue wraparound sarong showed off her luscious, tan shoulders against the room's white décor.

When a waitress approached with their menus, Bill ordered cocktails.

Mickey, facing the harbor with her back to the dining room, said, "Martinis. My heavens, are we girding for war?"

He peeked over his menu and saw Tray Robertson across the room, catching Bill's eye with a raised finger.

"Here he comes," Bill whispered.

Mickey buried her face in her menu.

"And the little fat one. He's getting up, too," Bill added.

The fat one looked ridiculous in his extra-extra large Honduran shirt coat, worn untucked in his favor. Made of roaring pink fabric, it cascaded over his midsection.

Tray looked cool in a crisp, light madras shirt and slacks.

Bill rose and held out his hand, trying for a smile that barely managed to appear. Mickey, though scared to death, wore a sincere smile.

"Good evening, Captain Tray," Bill said.

"Well, looky what we have here." Tray grinned as if they were long-lost cruising buddies. Shaking Bill's hand, he leaned over to buss Mickey's cheek. "Mickey, you look more beautiful than ever."

He almost grabbed her right hand with both of his. She felt a small piece of paper brush her palm, which she unobtrusively stuffed down her bra when no one was looking.

Tray gestured to his friend. "Hector, this is Mickey and Bill. This is my boss, the owner of the *Enchantress* out there, Mr. Hector Caraja."

The fat man asked, "Mickey, huh? Where they been hiding you, Beautiful?"

He made no attempt to recognize Bill or shake his hand, pushing past Tray to reach Mickey. "Trying to keep a gorgeous piece like you away from ol' Hector? You come to the yacht, Mickey. We gonna have a hurricane party."

Tray tried to pull Hector away and pushed Bill toward his own chair.

Mickey patted Bill's hand and gazed into Hector's eyes, saying sweetly, "Why, thank you, Hector. We just ordered. Maybe later?"

Tray hauled Hector away, weaving between tables, as they crossed the room toward the exit.

Mickey and Bill sat frozen, listening to the man's shouts all the way from the front door.

"Hey! I want that broad aboard the *Enchantress*, you hear me? Hear me?"

Mickey, looking at Bill, saw him doing a slow burn. With a wink, she said, "Let's see what the note fairy brought us this time."

She pulled out the note, scanned it, and handed it to Bill.

Bill,
 Tomorrow afternoon, likely all boats ordered off docks. Suggest follow us to hurricane hole, Allens-Pensacola Cay.
  Tray

The normally feathery, musky, prevailing southeasterly breeze in the early evening was nonexistent, though it was usually blocked by the lee created by Marsh Harbour. The wind, nevertheless, popped up to a steady, whistling moan of twenty to thirty knots northeast. It rattled the wooden louvers on the room's walls and blew out the candle on the dining table.

The louvers were promptly turned down and the candle relit, but the room, despite the lingering diners scattered throughout, turned quiet. Faces seemed to change with the weather, becoming flat and expressionless, avoiding eye contact across tables. The yachtsman-skippers, trying to appear nonchalant and casual, strained every few seconds with the rattling and banging louvers that hid the choppy harbor.

Mickey and Bill picked at their beautiful Bahamian lobster dinners. Both wondered just what the note meant and how Tray Robertson fit into the situation. Maybe he was sincerely trying to be helpful without blowing his cover. Maybe their appearance at the island placed him on a dangerous tightrope. Maybe he was just trying to make them think so.

Dinner dwindled into a stiff, strained silence against a background shuffled to the foreground, with the relentless approaching reality of Camellia.

"I'm sorry," Mickey said once they were outside. "This was all my idea."

They walked down the road toward the boat. The night sky was studded with stars, but the trees along the road groaned, their branches scraping and clawing at each other.

"I didn't put up much of an argument," Bill replied. "You got it together. I agreed, and I said I had to do this. I still feel that way."

She put her arm around his back, as they walked.

"I'll admit I didn't bargain for falling into their laps, and assuredly not for a hurricane."

"I think we should quit." She stopped abruptly. "We can anchor the boat behind an island or up a creek, dinghy in to shore, grab a cab to Green Turtle-Treasure Cay Airport, and fly out of here—if they're still flying tomorrow, and if we can get seats."

To get her walking again, he said, "Maybe you're right, but Casey Lee and I are doing our little deed in the morning at Barclays before I go anywhere."

★   ★   ★

The first light of dawn came to Marsh Harbour in the shape of an ugly wedge the color of a nasty bruise.

Bill slipped out of the forward cabin bunk. Mickey sighed as he moved, drifting in a pleasant dream.

He hadn't slept more than a couple hours, staring at the Bertram's headliner over the bunk, waiting, wanting to be dressed and ready when Casey Lee arrived. There was no telling how early he might con a pilot into taking off.

He pulled on his Levi's, a dark gray sweatshirt, boat shoes, and walked onto the dock. He always walked at home when he had to think. He tramped along, kicking the shit out of himself for lots of things, the schizo in his mind playing all the parts, as he beat up on himself. It was the inside against the outside, the devil's advocate against God-knew-whom.

He walked down Abaco Road away from the harbor, but he wasn't thinking anything. He felt impatient with the whole nightmare. Maybe it was actually fear that they already had him and were simply choosing the time and place.

You're afraid, aren't you, Sky King? he asked himself. *Different, isn't it, knowing in advance, unlike jumping and then discovering the screw-up too late and then learning you're going to be splattered?*

The black, blue, green, and yellow of dawn were gone. Gray bands of squall lines, like old, reefed sails, ran across the southern sky. He left no shadow, as he stumbled along.

The road was lumpy from constant patching, and he caught his heel on a pothole that jarred him back to his thoughts of Mickey. For the first time on their trip, she was the one who decided to have sex. She pushed it, as if trying to occupy his every minute. Feeling too distracted, he turned her down.

She said she didn't blame him.

There still hadn't been one word about money since they left Florida.

Absorbed in his thoughts and oblivious to his surroundings, he didn't see the cab barreling toward him in the wrong lane—the British way of driving. It skidded to a stop, throwing shell dust into the air, as the rear door flew open.

"Hey, Boy, you lost?"

Bill stared into the back seat, while the two passengers laughed hysterically.

"He sure don't look like no big-time citrus dude now, does he?" Casey Lee asked, laughing.

Mary Beth Holly crossed her long, thin legs to make more room. Bill squeezed in between them and turned to her. She was the same as when they had dinner at her home that night, looking beautiful, controlled, and cool.

"Thanks, you two," Bill managed.

CHAPTER TWELVE
MANANA AT WHALE CAY PASSAGE

Bill and Casey Lee stood across the street from Barclays Bank at 9:00 A.M. Light bands of windblown rain swept the area every few minutes. They wore foul-weather jackets, and Bill carried his sailor's duffle half full of wadded newspaper.

They looked like nervous yachtsmen ashore on hurried, now pointless, errands, nervously awaiting the next weather bulletin. In another place and time, they would have looked like bank robbers, but there, they were perfect.

"Ask to get into your safe deposit box. The clerk will ask your name and pull your signature card. Sign your name. If your signature is already on the card above where you sign, which wouldn't surprise me, match their version as closely as possible. Got it?"

Casey Lee nodded. "Forge my own signature."

"Got ID just in case?"

"Got it all—driver's license, voter card, copy of my birth certificate, and passport."

"Passport?"

"Yeah. Trent was gonna take me to South America to look at cattle."

"You didn't go?"

"Tray went supposedly in the summer of last year."

They looked at each other and knew exactly where and when he went.

"Let's hit it." Bill indicated Casey Lee should precede him. "Act like it's old-home week."

They walked into Barclays Bank as if they were two Southern boys who owned the place. The bank personnel unknowingly witnessed two things about Casey Lee Christy—he could pick a name off a brass nameplate and assign it to a face in half a second, and he could do it at fifty paces.

He sauntered down the length of the bank, past balustrades on the left and teller's cages on the right and correctly pinned each name to a face.

"Good morning, Edith," he said to an ink-black, 250-pound assistant cashier.

"Morning, Smith. Morning, Deborah. Mr. Bethel, how are you? Basil, my boy."

All the employees felt embarrassed they didn't know the customer's name, because he obviously knew theirs. Barclays prided itself on that.

Basil, a young, Black, rail-thin man in a starched white shirt too big in the collar, stood behind the cage labeled *Safe Deposit Boxes.*

"Basil," Casey Lee said, "I'd like to get into my box before the weather hits, if I may."

"I'm sorry, Sir."

Bill and Casey Lee froze.

"I've forgotten your name."

"Christy, Casey Lee Christy. By the way, I was talking to, oh, you know who I mean..." He snapped his fingers over his shoulder. "It was just the other day."

Basil stepped to the file.

"Cooper Hannah," Bill said clearly.

"Yes," Casey Lee continued. "I was talking to Cooper Hannah the other day. He seems pleased with you and has his eye on you."

Basil returned with the signature card.

Casey Lee began writing his name. The previous signatures, directly above where he was writing, were perfect.

Basil watched the pen move, as Casey Lee wrote. Bill hoped he was contemplating advancement under Cooper Hannah's watchful eye. Maybe he would go to Nassau or even London.

"Very good, Sir. Your key, please."

Casey Lee looked up, suddenly stricken, and put his hand to his mouth. Patting his pockets, he slowly turned to Bill.

"You didn't," Bill said in utter disgust. "You forgot your key?"

Basil considered this problem. Casey Lee and Bill felt as if time stopped.

"I can have the lock drilled out and assign you a new box, Mr. Christy. However, we must charge for the service. It's one hundred dollars, I'm afraid. This isn't uncommon."

Bill felt as if the entire bank heard him exhale.

"Fine, Basil," Casey Lee said without flinching. "Good thinking."

"I'll call the locksmith. It might take awhile, what with the weather."

"Tell him it's important. Tell you what." Casey Lee lowered his voice. "There's a fifty-dollar tip in it for him and for you, plus the $100 fee. How's that?"

Basil backed toward his desk and its phone while shaking his head. He raised his hands to deflect even the idea of a tip, but he smiled.

In minutes, though it felt like hours, the locksmith arrived, and thirty seconds of drilling out the tiny lock began. Basil opened an adjacent safe-deposit box and handed Casey Lee the key. Casey Lee slipped him two $100 bills, and the young banker left the vault.

At the door, Basil asked, "What about the other gentlemen, Mr. Christy? Will there be other lessees or deputized signatures?"

Casey Lee and Bill eyed each other.

With infinite casualness, Casey Lee turned and said, "Naw, Basil. You treat me so well, I'm gonna make it a point to be around more and handle things myself. I won't need any other signatures at this time."

Basil grinned, saluted his customer, and stepped out. He hadn't remembered Mr. Christy's name before that morning, but he would remember it from then on.

Bill opened the drilled-out door and turned it flush against the wall. Together, they slid out the one-and-a-half by two-foot container and set it on the adjacent courtesy viewing counter and opened the lid.

On top was a black savings account book. Under it, neatly banded, were packs of large bills. Bill estimated they were worth $10,000 each.

Casey Lee slowly shook his head. Bill reached down along the front of the box to the bottom, estimating how many layers, then dragged a finger across the top to count how many packs.

"What we got here, Bull?" Casey Lee asked quietly.

Looking incredulously at his friend, Bill whispered, "There's more than two million in this box."

The savings account book showed a balance of nearly $100,000. Logged in it were irregularly timed, sizable deposits and regular, large withdrawals. Stuck in the back and folded were receipted, executed wire transfer orders that matched most of the withdrawals, transfers to banks in Nassau, the Caymans, Geneva, and London. Millions had passed through that account while the balance always hovered around $100,000.

They pulled the new box from its slot and swapped it for the full one, closed the lid on all that money and the little black book, closed the lock door, and called for Basil.

Basil came in with the lessee's copy of the rental contract for the new safe-deposit box, along with the only spare key, and gave them to Casey Lee. He turned the new key in the lock, then the bank's key, locking away over two million dollars from everyone on earth except himself.

He stared at the two keys in his hand.

"Bet you won't lose keys no more, Mon, aye, Mr. Christy?" Basil asked.

Casey Lee nodded, then they left the bank exactly as he entered. Ambling past the teller's cages, he tipped his imaginary hat to every Bahama mama, pointed a finger and winked at one Black face after another, always using the right name in each case. In passing, he even hustled Edith for a dinner date.

"One of these nights, Edith," he said. "One of these nights, Mama."

Her whole body gushed with laughter, and she shooed the two men out with her fat little hands waving in the air.

Outside the bank, where the young employees were quickly fastening hurricane shutters on the glass façade, all signs of jubilation evaporated.

The look of Marsh Harbour changed. The sky was an intense, bright white, blazing and blaring down, an effect of having the sun appear to be everywhere overhead, creating a gauzy, brilliant scrim over all. The sun burned down through a crystal clear, extreme high pressure upper-level air down through a thin, translucent marine layer that moved at an alarming rate of speed. It was the outermost wind associated with the extended, far-reaching edge of the giant dome of the storm that measured over 300 miles in diameter.

Camellia was coming.

The U.S. Weather Bureau's noon update came:

Effective immediately: Status Hurricane
Camellia upgraded from Hurricane Watch to
Warning.

Worried Abaconians and tourists all over the Bahamas hovered over their VHF radios, staring at the frozen, cow-eyed faces of friends and family. Yachtsmen and crews hustled to get their boats away from the docks and somehow sheltered in creeks and backwaters. Vessels in lagoons lowered storm anchors well away from others, free to drag long distances anywhere except docks, where pilings would destroy hulls and vice versa.

The citizens of Marsh Harbour, the birthplace of most of them, eyed the strange, exploded sky and foreign, oily waters and backed away as if from an apparition. Faces ashen, they ran for home in panic.

Back at the boat, Her Majesty's Customs Officer Matthew was gone, but he stayed long enough to help Mickey rearrange the mooring lines for a quick cast-off, looping them once around the big dock cleats before cleating them back aboard.

She already had the engines warmed up and running. On the bridge, Mary Beth wore a foul-weather jacket and shorts. She'd zipped the clear enclosure panels around the bimini top except for astern, as ordered.

Bill first, then Casey Lee, dropped to the Bertram's gunwale, then the aft deck. Bill tossed the empty duffel in a corner and ran up the bridge ladder.

"Get your banking all done, Captain?" Mary Beth asked.

Though he wasn't in a mood for games, Bill winked at her. "Whoever they are, they're broke now."

"Whoever they are? Come on, Captain. Remind me to give you a big kiss for that soon. By the way, I've been sitting up here, watching the *Enchantress.* My rather large Bahamian friend, Roosevelt Awbrey, is aboard."

Below, Casey Lee stepped to the salon door. Inside the galley, Mickey secured for a rough passage. She hooked all the cabinet doors and the fridge and barely heard the door open and close behind her.

"Well? Was it what you thought it would be?" she asked, her back to the door.

"Yes, Ma'am," a voice drawled.

She whirled around. "Oh, I'm sorry. I thought you were…"

"You're…Mickey."

"You're…Casey Lee," she finished almost in a whisper.

She stared, as did he. Oddly, they'd never met. As they stared, they tried to cope with the sexual waves moving between them.

Finally, he extended his hand. She meant to shake it and let go, but she held on. As they touched, she looked into the eyes of a panther, as they'd been recently described to her, and felt excitingly naked.

Finally, they noticed they were still shaking hands, but they didn't know what else to do.

"Well, do you have a last name, Mickey?"

"It's Morgan-Lloyd, hyphenated."

"From?"

"Palm Beach, Florida."

"That's always your home?"

"My family's lived there for fifty years."

"Mickey Morgan-Lloyd," he said slowly. "Miss Mickey Morgan-Lloyd of Palm Beach, Florida. Whew-ee."

"Whew-ee what?"

"That sure is a name."

Casey Lee Christy, she thought, tasting his eyes again.

Muffled thumps and thuds on deck drummed through the headliner, as Mary Beth took in a bow line.

The intercom suddenly said, "Mickey, free the spring and stern lines. We're getting the hell outta here."

Mickey punched the button on the galley phone. "Yes, Sir. Right away. We're all squared away down here." Her hand trembled, as she hung up.

Backing, they cleared the outer slip pilings. The port clutch went to reverse, the starboard went forward, and the thirty-five-footer rotated counterclockwise ninety degrees to face the channel.

At the helm, Bill gave the docks 100 yards clearance at no-wake speed and firewalled both throttles.

He looked astern and saw, in their dwindling wake 500 yards away, the bow of a motor yacht. Her bow cutwater spread out in a wide, five-foot-high white wave on each side, and her stern was dug into the water. She showed high-performance power without any respect for the harbor.

The binoculars clarified any question he might have. It was the *Enchantress.*

★　★　★

Two hundred miles east-northeast of Turks and Caicos Islands and infatuated with the 3,000-foot ocean depths near the island's escarpment, Camellia was a living thing gone mad.

She held course, riding the Trade Winds across the Atlantic to near Barbados, scaring the Barbadians half to death before veering northwest on a course of 300 degrees. She skirted the Windwards, the Leewards, and the southernmost of the Bahamas Archipelago with precision, following a perfectly straight course since her turn seventy-two hours previously.

Such a precise course frightened the authorities, because the northeastern escarpment of Eleuthera and the Abacos lay at an angle of 320 degrees. Without a change in bearing, collision was inevitable. The escarpment wasn't going to move, and the odds of Camellia altering course narrowed with every forward movement.

Under her broad, 300-mile-wide span, the sea had no surface, water and sky no separation. There was only a dark, indistinguishable maelstrom, a gray-water Medusa. Her tentacles curved out and hung, poised to sting in every direction. Around her boneless, jellied body, she scooped up froth, spun it, and spat it out on her northwest quadrant in liquid mountains to form tidal waves.

*   *   *

Enchantress' owner, Hector Caraja, in the main salon, gave the orders before, and nothing happened. He couldn't trust Captain Tray, but Rosey, he thought, came with built-in loyalty. After all, he created an automaton out of the big Black man, trained him to hassle the importers, hustle the loads, jockey the planes, deal with dealers, and walk in fucking front doors of fucking Swiss banks without knowing what kind of fucking reception he would receive. It was better than doing it himself.

Marsh Harbour wasn't an ideal place for a double hit to take out Burton and the babe, Hector realized, what with all the action in the harbor. He understood why he fucked up badly back there.

Hector had only one reason to stay aboard, which was to pop the Burton kid, especially after he started poking his nose into things. Otherwise, Hector Caraja would have walked or even run up the dock at the mention of a storm. Boats were a dime a dozen. He would rather have gone to the airport and paid some slob to fly him to Miami.

Just before they cast off, he gave the orders once again. Sitting in his bathrobe, he said, "Rosey, bring up the AR-15. Captain, when they pull out, do the same. In the passage out around Whale Cay, get near 'em, maybe 150 yards back. Rosey, you take out the front porch. We get outside Whale Cay, put a magazine into the Burton kid, and make a sieve outta that hull."

Tray and Rosey looked at each other.

"You don't understand," Tray pleaded. "There will be other boats using Whale Cay Passage, all running from the storm, Hector."

"We got more magazines, the BAR, and a few grenades. Your yachting friends got all that, Captain?"

Rosey had hoped to talk Mr. No Wet out of getting rid of Tray after the Burton deal, but Tray was blowing any chance he had of surviving by arguing.

"Even if we hit him at the helm," Tray said, "one of those two girls aboard can drive."

"Two girls now?"

"Yes. One just joined them—Mary Beth Holly. You met Mickey already. She can drive, too."

"Mickey, yeah, the beautiful black-haired bitch, right? The other one good lookin'?"

Tray realized he'd said the wrong thing. "Yeah."

"We take the two chicks aboard, then we sink the fucker. Let's go." Hector, shooing them from the salon, made another starter at the bar, his third.

Rosey went to the engine room to get the AR-15 from its hidden locker, a false bank of batteries that had been gutted to create a storage place.

As Rosey returned, Hector called him into the salon again. From his chair, he said quietly, "About Robertson. Wait till after the storm. We need him to get this thing to Allans-Pensacola Cay."

What we need, Rosey thought, *is to get out through Whale Cay Passage and around that huge rock formation before the place turns into a rage.*

It was the exact image of a huge, surfacing whale. If they were in the northwest channel end, they should be safe.

Every knowledgeable seaman respected Whale Cay Passage, the most dangerous in all the Bahamas. Port side, beside the island cay, were wild currents even on the best of days. Erosion carved deep, blue, subsurface caves around the jagged corner.

On the starboard side, across the passage, waited Loggerhead Bars. On the chart it was just a half-mile-diameter reef. In reality, a huge, jagged mass barely inches below the surface threatened the edge of the channel. Rosey had seen cargo freighters dead in that passage, gashed beyond hope, hanging vertically down, their sterns buoyed by trapped air. It was impassable at any time. The shallow leeward water inside the Sound was navigable only by small, shallow-draft boats. All that was instinctive to Rosey.

"Mr. No Wet, forget it for now." He gestured with the rifle. "We got to worry about ourselves. The storm isn't funny. Whale Cay Passage gets too rough for *Enchantress.* It's the only way out. We run now, or we're caught dead. You don't know."

"I never seen Allans-Pensacola before. Rosey, how 'bout you build me another drink?" He apparently hadn't heard a word Rosey said.

Rosey looked at his boss in disgust without glancing at the bar. The little fat man snapped his fingers and pointed with his glass.

For the first time, Rosey had enough. He turned and walked forward, going up the bridge ladder.

Hector stood, straightened his bathrobe, and lurched toward the bar. Three fingers of rum on the rocks would improve his sea legs. It would taste better made firsthand, too.

★　★　★

Mickey, as navigator, stood beside Bill and pointed toward the area of Loggerhead Bars, ten degrees off starboard. Rather, she pointed to where it should be. It was submerged under the rising tide and the ocean's five-foot chop. To port, she grimaced at the cay's jagged corner, where whitewater ripped like rapids. Bill maneuvered to enter the passage and slowed to seven knots to handle the bow seas.

Enchantress drew up within 100 yards. Tray, skippering the larger boat, came down from the bridge to the enclosed pilothouse lower station, where it was much drier. He watched through the windshield as Rosey, with the AR-15, tried to negotiate the foredeck.

The big Bahamian knelt with his elbow on the port deck box, trying to aim. The foredeck yawed and rose on the crests, then crashed into the valleys. Green water flooded the deck. He couldn't hold even the entire Bertram in his sights, much less the figure at the helm. It was insanity to watch his target swing through his sights.

He gave up and turned back to the pilothouse, groping on the glistening deck for the lifelines. The greatest diver in the Islands was gasping when he finally reached the pilothouse open door.

In the salon, Hector gave up clutching his bathrobe and sat with white knuckles on the chair arms, trying not to get thrown against the bulkhead. He listened for the rattle of the AR-15, but nothing came. Then he heard the Captain and Rosey yelling at each other.

Rosey, sopping wet and furious, cursed and shouted alternately in his Bahamian and British accents. "Absolutely no way, Mon. Stupid, I say."

"Wait until we come back in at the northwest end!" Tray shouted, but Rosey didn't hear him.

Rosey, in the open pilothouse door, caught movement in the corner of his eye that was nearly abeam. Freezing, he stared into the erupting distance for a second, then catapulted into Tray at the doorway, pointing and shaking his rod-straight arm out to starboard. The thing was less than 2,000 feet away, ten degrees off the starboard bow.

Tray saw it, and his eyes bulged, his mouth open.

The huge Bahamian whirled on his shipmate, giving an order through clenched teeth. "Jump! Jump!" He roared a third time, "Jump, for God's sake!"

He threw Tray athwart ship out to the rail and followed, nearly climbing the man's back at the lifelines. They stared at the racing mountain of foam below, coming off the bow wake. Hector Caraja bellowed from the salon, demanding a report.

A split second later, in the silent blur of their bodies, there was nothing but the hiss of compression in their ears.

★   ★   ★

Aboard the Bertram's bridge, Bill got a glimpse. He concentrated on taking the seas ten degrees off their bow.

"Get in a rhythm with them," Mickey said. "Feel, don't just see."

She spotted movement, too, and saw the big Bahamian jump, followed by Tray. Both vanished instantly into the water.

Bill felt and heard a rumble, then he saw something through the windshield, like a surreal horizon slowly lifting. Was it a wall of fog, a strange cloud, a mirage?

What came from his mouth was, "Fog. Fog out there. You see fog? That's not fog! Rogue? Tidal wave? Tsunami?"

Then he screamed, "Mickey!"

She repeated his words verbatim as if she heard his babbling lunacy, then she saw his horrified expression and looked in the direction of his gaze.

"Jesus Christ!" she shouted, grabbing the wheel. "Helm to port! Port!" She pulled hand over hand, spinning the wheel counterclockwise.

Bill regained his senses and took over.

"Hurry!" she said. "Lee shore. Right. Shit. Hurry, Man! See the Casuarinas?"

"What?"

"The trees!" She pointed ahead.

"Beach. Run for it!" She whirled to face the oncoming horror. "Firewall it!"

The hull veered to port, leaving the whale-shaped rock behind. They were airborne each time the beam seas dropped from under the keel. The boat soared, roared, fell, and bit into the water repeatedly. Green water over the bow burst against the bridge windshield.

Mickey, climbing over the wheel, slammed the throttles against the console and held them down. The engines screamed like a madhouse under them, while on top, they hung on for their lives.

Finally, they slid under the lee of the southeast point of Whale Cay, which broke the seas. Wave crests merged, valleys shallowed. The props stayed under, caught, and shot the boat onto a plane flat out, the tachs locked in sync with both engines redlined.

Mickey kept staring at the passage, watching *Enchantress,* which was incredibly still heading out. They had to be on autopilot.

"Jesus Christ!" she shouted.

The seventy-two-foot yacht passed beyond Whale Cay's east point into the open ocean, spray flying and disappeared behind the huge rock outcropping of Whale Cay.

⋆   ⋆   ⋆

Hector Caraja almost didn't see it, though he had a box seat. There was no response to his shouts, so he lurched forward over *Enchantress'* shifting cabin sole, wedged himself into the pilothouse doorway to straighten out those goddamn boys of his, then stared incomprehensibly at the empty pilothouse. When he called their names, there was no answer.

He focused on the four-foot-diameter wheel that jerked to port, then starboard, back and forth, as if the captain was still steering. The ship dived into a valley that increased her speed wildly. For a beat, she seemed stable.

Hector timed it, jumped for the wheel, and grabbed it with both hands. It jerked his arms back and forth. He strained to see ahead, castigating the lousy captain for not wiping down the condensation on the windshield.

He watched in childlike amazement, as the condensation rose like Niagara Falls, turned upside down, and became a towering, green-gray canyon wall arching toward him with smoke billowing from the rim.

Enchantress broached to port, as the sea went out from under her. Her port sponsons tripped her and laid the seventy-two footer on her side with spinning props. She rose on water curving vertically up through its own pipeline, helplessly found her slot on the glassy curl, and shot the tube like a surfer. The wave, a liquid mountain over fifty-feet high, broke its back approaching the shallows, and a frothing, careening crest engulfed the boat.

Eight million tons of water moving at ninety miles an hour smashed against Whale Cay's rock face in a thunderous, vibrating explosion that shook the sea like a quake. Hector Caraja, the last to see it, saw what the surfers called "pure stoke" before the world went white, then black.

* * *

The little Bertram sat on the opposite, protected side, in the lee, having literally reversed course. It was almost directly among the Casuarina trees, barely awash, wedged in a tiny cove of white sand, while they watched.

At first there was total silence, as giant geysers exploded over Whale Cay's hills. Then diamond-colored balloons rose, only to crash on the leeward slopes and run into Abaco Sound. Midflight came the ear-blowing sound of hideous, vibrating moans, followed by echoing, rhythmic thunder, like the sound of clusters of bombs exploding on a beach.

Shock sent ten-foot waves across Abaco Sound. Water poured into the Sound from both passages, ten-foot-deep rivers above the actual surface. Their white, foaming headwaters collided, and the waterfronts of Abaco Sound flooded.

The Bertram crew waded across the deck through Casuarina branches and piles of long, brown needles, with saltwater everywhere. Looks passed among the four, and, reaching instantaneous consensus, they cranked up the engines and flat-sticked them again, praying like hell for Green Turtle.

Mary Beth glanced back at Whale Cay, already less distinguishable, turning gray in mist beyond their wake. Mickey saw her looking after and turned, too. For Mickey, Whale Cay's lack of charitableness was ancient history. Charts and cruising guides always mark it with special *CAUTION* in bold print, warning captains to avoid the Passage in heavy weather.

"This will finish Trent Robertson," Mary Beth said above the roar.

Though she couldn't hear her, she watched Mickey's mouth form the words, "God save their souls."

Mickey remembered something else about that place. There were legends told by old native fishermen and divers who considered Whale Cay Passage sacrosanct. The Bahamians talked about it. Supposedly, somewhere under Whale Cay's east point, the tidal currents continued an excavation begun in the Pleistocene.

Down six fathoms, a sand vein in the limestone gave way and opened. Seawater enlarged the cave. Countless rages on the hill above opened a fissure, eventually enough to let in light. They say the ceiling took the shape of a cloister dome, and the place attracted life, including coral, giant jewfish, parrotfish, lobster, morays, and sharks. The cave entrance, under a ledge at the bottom, was said to be found because of a glow from the cave's dome, which gave the place a grotto effect of sky blue.

Old-time professional spear fishermen, when they were in trouble and caught in tidal rips, bitten, stung, wounded, or ill, were said to use it. Understandably, they considered it a blessed place and told their youngsters about it.

According to the story, divers had to go straight to the bottom and enter at the blue light, then swim up inside, toward the silvery surface until they broke through under the dome and found themselves breathing air and still alive.

CHAPTER THIRTEEN
GREEN TURTLE CAY, CURTAIN OF BACKLIT RASPBERRY

It was just seven nautical miles to Green Turtle. The Bertram plunged and bucked north.

On the bridge, Casey Lee and Bill were lashed to the helm with a mooring line, fighting the wheel by hand. Autopilot was worthless in such seas.

The waters of Abaco Sound ricocheted off every rock and shore. Waves collided, exploding upward like water jostled in a bucket. The sea churned, becoming unreadable, a milky-green chowder of debris, twigs, and branches. Wild winds came out of nowhere—hot, cold with slashing rain, fifty and gusting, shrieking, then gone. Long, swollen clouds with blue-black bellies raced westward at frightening clips. The tiny cays and rocks between islands disappeared. Noname Cay, between Whale Cay and Green Turtle, was a cloud of froth.

They watched the tachometers swing wildly every time the props left the water. Walls of water broke over the bimini top with every lunge and dive. Their speed through the water jerked from fifteen to twenty knots to fifteen to thirty, while speed over the bottom was a foot at a time.

Green Turtle remained a misty, dark mound on the horizon.

Thank God, a mound, Bill thought. *A mound is a hill, and a hill will be enough.*

Green Turtle offered the highest elevation in the Northern Bahamas, as high as eighty-odd feet above sea level. In the lee of those hills was protection.

All Mary Beth, Casey Lee, Mickey, and Bill had to do was hang on until the picture-postcard little town of New Plymouth was on their beam. The town occupied the island's south tip, and north from there, the elevation rose. All they had to do was get there and slide under that leeward shield.

Below, the women were buffeted off their feet. They sat on cushions on the cabin sole, their backs braced against the aft bulkhead. Neither tried to speak, riding with the punches, trying to blot out the violent noises and terrible pounding of the boat under maximum stress.

Mickey turned her head away, embarrassed, realizing the two hadn't talked since Mary Beth and Casey Lee arrived. *Some welcome,* she thought.

Bill told her that Mary Beth had solid firsthand but circumstantial evidence of drug running. Mickey wondered what Mary Beth knew about her.

She was about to say something, anything, when Mary Beth blurted, "I saw them jump, both of them." She was in tears.

"I know, Mary Beth. I saw it, too. I was looking right at them."

"They drowned, didn't they?"

Mickey sighed. "I would imagine."

With that, Mary Beth seemed to get hold of herself and took a deep breath, though it was filled with nervous shudders. Fighting her way past that, she offered a smile as if in apology.

Mickey watched that extraordinarily beautiful, sophisticated woman, far out of her element in the present madness, dab her eyes and regain her composure. It was impressive.

"I met Roosevelt Awbrey on a date with Tray," Mary Beth said. "Tray insisted I meet him at a redneck bar, the Palms, before going out for dinner."

"The Bahamian was at the bar with Tray, like buddies?" Mickey didn't get an answer, so she asked, "You dated Tray Robertson?"

"Once. He had the town snowed, except he was his biggest fan."

"Rings a bell."

"Tray suggested they put Casey Lee in Burton Groves as manager. He said his little brother would keep his mouth shut and do as he was told. The translation was, 'It's my territory. I know it. I'll handle it.' Like the kid was his slave. He was trying to tell some very scary people what to do. He put Casey Lee in danger without even a hint to his brother. I got interested at that point but not in Tray. Then there was the envelope..."

"Wait, wait, wait! Casey Lee Christy and Tray Robertson are family?"

"No, Mickey. Tray's father took Casey Lee in when he was a kid and pretty much raised him. The boss, Hector Caraja, sent Rosey Awbrey up to tell Tray no dice. They wanted their own man in that spot. I had to sit through the whole thing. I didn't know what it meant at the time, of course. We didn't go out for dinner. I can tell you that much."

The information and chronology whirled through Mickey's head, dropping efficiently into memory slots.

They felt the boat slow down. Well in the lee, they produced a discernible wake again.

Mary Beth looked out the starboard port. "You know what Tray told me?" She leaned against the glass and squinted out, staring over the edge of their stern wake as far as she could see. "Roosevelt Awbrey was the best diver in the Bahamas."

Something in Mary Beth's tone made Mickey get up to join her. Mary Beth's focus was far aft, where the wake dissolved into distant gray, as if she could see all the way back to Whale Cay Passage. Mickey looked at the woman's face, wondering if she could see old divers teaching their sons the sacred legends.

"Ladies, look out starboard," the intercom said.

The voice sounded relieved.

Mickey grabbed the wall phone, still looking out. "New Plymouth. We're proud of you boys." She hung up the phone and pointed, so Mary Beth would look. Mickey was ready to extol the picturesqueness of the 19th-century town, with its narrow streets, rows of neat, pastel cottages with flower boxes, when Mary Beth tapped the port and pointed.

"They look like tombstones," Mary Beth said.

Mickey saw there was no one on the deserted streets, and all the houses were shuttered.

Bill stared at the water in confusion. There were no channel markers. While Casey Lee steered them at Slow/Forward, Bill hovered over the chart book for Green Turtle.

Green Turtle was unique. Besides the rare, protective hills and harbor, there were two sounds. Black Sound was off their starboard quarter, while the other sound, north of them, was called White Sound. Between the two, a blunt peninsula with a very prominent hill jutted out from the starboard shore, forming separate entrances.

He put his finger on the starburst chart symbol labeled *Hill* and read its elevation at fifty feet. Looking to his right, he saw it. Forward, not more than a mile, was the highest hill on the island, Big Bluff, at eighty-three feet, wrapping around White Sound like a horseshoe. The east slope rambled down to the ocean, while the west slope was a sheer rock face plunging into Abaco Sound.

He looked at Big Bluff through the binocs and at the cluster of light-yellow buildings on its crest. "Bluff House Resort is dead ahead, Casey Lee, at the top of the hill." He offered the binoculars, but Casey Lee ignored them.

Casey Lee's eyes tensed, as he searched for movement among the buildings that were still too far away. Maybe a doorway changed shape, bulged briefly, and maybe not. It was hard to tell. The occupants might have closed up and run to safety.

Had he seen slight movement? The possible figure shadowed in a doorway at Bluff House was too faint to see clearly. It looked like a man stepping forward. His carriage was that of a gentleman, maybe an official, someone with a military background. He dressed like a Bahamian fisherman in dirty pants cut off at the knees, no shirt or shoes.

The man stared through his Zeiss binoculars at the tiny Bertram, a small speck one mile south, approaching the narrow, markerless channel. He'd been watching since it emerged from the mist near Noname Cay.

He hid in the doorway that opened the clubhouse onto the cantilevered redwood deck. A large, railed platform surrounded the pool and hung over the edge of the hill that dropped into Abaco Sound. The view was among the most breathtaking in the Bahamas.

He held a VHF microphone with a spiral cord trailing to an inside, wall-mounted transceiver. Pushing the button, he said, "Yacht approaching White Sound, Bluff House calling."

He paused before clicking the button again. "Captain Charles Schneider, Bluff House. Come back."

On the bridge, Bill slowed the boat, as they came abeam of the hill that separated White Sound from Black Sound and picked up the microphone.

Mickey, below, reached to grab the lower station mic, as the bridge mic keyed. She stepped onto the deck to see what Bill would do.

He shrugged. *Charles Schneider?* he wondered.

Mickey smiled to herself. That was Bill.

Another set of binoculars watched the Bertram, held motionless on the crest of the fifty-foot hill that separated the two Sounds. The young Black boy sat in a pile of dead coral that matched his color. His elbows were on his knees, the binoculars to his eyes. He had the advantage of a down angle on the Bertram.

The woman on the aft deck came into focus. She was White, a beautiful woman with jet-black hair. He recognized her from the Jack Tar. After a moment, she stepped back inside.

He recognized the boat. Two men were on the bridge, their backs to him. The unfamiliar one covered the other man.

The other man turned and looked directly into the boy's binoculars. It was the man in the car at the stateside airport, the guy in the Jack Tar lobby.

The binoculars fell and slapped against his chest. His head sagged until the eye cups pushed against his eye sockets. If those men were in the harbor, then his father was dead. He knew Mr. No Wet would have him killed without a thought.

In his mind, he heard a voice say, *Remember, Winston T. Awbrey, from whence you come.*

He had to find a radio, to try again.

Bill pressed the transmit button and said, "Bluff House, this is yacht approaching. Switch channel?"

"Roger. Name it."

"Channel six-eight?"

"Roger. Six-eight."

He changed channels. "Go."

"Yes, Captain. Welcome to Bluff House. Have suggestions on navigating White Sound Channel. How on that?"

"Roger. Go."

"The markers are submerged, obviously. You're right about over the outer one at the moment. The inner channel marker, a white pyramid, still has the tip above the water."

"Can't see it, Bluff House."

"Not yet. Split the shorelines. Come right up the middle slowly. At the marker, ease ten degrees to port. It's fifteen feet of water, but watch the flotsam. Came in a bit ago myself. How on that?"

"Roger, Bluff House. Thank you. Who's speaking, please? Over."

There was silence for a few seconds.

"You might repeat to your lovely crew the words, 'The Jack Tar did not survive.' She'll know."

Below on the Bertram, Mickey heard the words and raised her eyes to the heavens, her hands pressed together in front of her. "Regis!"

When he arrived at Bluff House, Regis stated there was trouble at the Jack Tar, and he ran for it. Kitty and Pearce Coady, the resort's owners, didn't need to hear more. They understood.

The tourism press called the couple, *hoteliers without peer.* Legendary, they played active roles in Bahamian culture, art, history, economy, and ecology. They knew about the cancers sweeping through their Bahamas. Keen perception was the secret ingredient at Bluff House.

"Regis Willoughby," Kitty said, speaking for both of them, "we're delighted as usual. God knows, we need the help."

Regis knew a lot, and the Coadys had their own special ways, unique but successful. He performed every task they asked—fishing-diving guide, busboy, dishwasher, cook, even relief maître d', which was usually the owner's job, and bartender.

At four o'clock, Regis stood at the doorway to the deck, staring through his binoculars. "Boat down there broadside to the channel," he reported to the owners.

"Well, Regis, bring 'em in."

The Bertram cleared the inner marker, and Regis directed them to a mooring buoy, where they tried to tie up. He sent out busboys in the sixteen-foot launch to help. When lines were doubled fore and aft, the four from the boat piled into the launch with their luggage, including, not that surprising even there, two hard suitcases.

When they arrived at the dock, Mickey leaped into Regis' arms, nearly knocking him over. "Regis! Dear God, I love you! The sound of your voice out there was such a relief."

Introductions were made with the four who clustered around the reserved Bahamian. Finally, they headed up the hill, the two boys following, each with a duffel and dragging a rock-hard suitcase.

Up on Big Bluff, the boys branched off and walked around back. The rest followed Regis through the front door into the main lounge, a soft-white, comfortable living room with ample, deep-cushioned couches and chairs, all in peaceful sea foam and peach tones. The so-called clubhouse, beautifully and professionally decorated, was more like a casual first-class Caribbean-style residential home. The southwest corner and west wall were made of tall, white-framed French windows and doors overlooking a large wooden deck. Beyond was Abaco Sound.

"Ah, our yachtsmen!"

They turned to see a middle-aged, vibrant man with a ruddy-tan face who bounded into the room. "Welcome. Delighted you got here."

Both women smiled at the cute man. He had receding, sandy hair in a crew cut, white slacks, and a navy blazer with impressive yachting crest—obviously a sailor.

"Pearce Coady." He changed to cordial host. "You kids look like you could use a shower and a drink. Regis?" He gestured to the French doors. "Cocktails are at six-thirty, rain or shine, war or peace, tranquility or...Camellia. Would you point the way, Regis?"

Regis went out the door and down the steps, then took a right and led the group the length of the wooden deck, toward a pair of abutting units painted the customary yellow and white, facing the pool.

Mickey eyed the sky, especially the meteorological show in the west, and asked, "Regis, these folks know there's a hurricane out there, don't they?"

"But of course, Ma'am."

She shook her head. "He's dressed like he's going to his club for dinner."

"Yes, Ma'am." He stepped forward, gesturing to their rooms. "That's exactly what he's doing."

All four walked to the first door, with a polished brass 5 on it and a hanging basket of flowers. Regis opened the door.

Mary Beth shrugged and stepped inside. On the left luggage rack was Bill's duffel, while Mary Beth's suitcase was on the right. In the middle was a queen double. Out the large window was a view that Mary Beth felt, had the weather been better, and if there really was justice and there was a God—especially if she had a certain man—could be very nice.

Mickey took one look, gave an identical shrug, and said, "We'll straighten it out later." She marched to room four.

At six-fifteen, people gathered in the lounge. Far above the roof, charcoal-gray ropes lay across the sky, crawling low and fast over Big Bluff's summit. In the distant west, under a musky scrim raised just above the horizon, a curtain of backlit raspberry rained down onto Great Abaco Island.

Throughout the Western Atlantic, including Bluff House, the six o'clock advisory was taken down verbatim:

Advisory #75 Hurricane Camellia:

Hurricane Warnings continue for Bahamas. Persons in this area should continue preparations for hurricane-force winds and abnormally high tides. Strong, extremely high seas and high tides affecting the east coasts of Exumas, Eleuthera, and Abacos, producing strong breaking surf of 20-50 foot waves. All persons within the Hurricane Warning area are advised to evacuate or move to higher ground.

In red waistcoat over starched white shirt with black bowtie, Regis was amused. If one had to work and be away from one's family serving one's homeland in such a situation, this certainly was the place, and cocktail hour was the time. He poured a double shot of his preferred island-made

Matusalem Rum. With it hidden between thumb and forefingers, knocked it back as innocent as a yawn. He smiled as he stood near the bar, watching the master at work—Pearce Coady, *raconteur.*

Whether the guest was at the bar panting or clear across the room, conversation hopping, the Number-One Bartender sought the order, prepared and delivered it, each with words of welcome, cheer, endearment, and a dissertation on the six-o'clock advisory. He did it endlessly until the first round was served to two dozen guests, including the four from the Bertram. More visitors were expected throughout the night if the local folk left their homes. They would be welcome.

Hostess Kitty oversaw the passing of hors d'oeuvres, conch strips marinated in lime juice and gin, lobster chunks, and stone crab claws with homemade dip. She talked animatedly with some, sympathetically with others, and passed eye signals to her husband about who needed what.

When host and hostess agreed that balance was achieved, the bar, not without ceremony, was relinquished to Regis. Studying the faces, he had to admit that in half an hour, the mood had elevated.

Mickey, who one male guest described as "the dark-haired lovely off the Bertram," caught Regis' eye by pointing at her wine glass, then held up her hand to indicate she'd come to him.

He thought she was quite attractive that night at the Jack Tar, and equally so the present evening.

She swished as she moved in her sheer pantsuit, accented with simple pearls. "Good evening," she said with a casual smile. "White, please, Regis."

He smiled and poured. She took the glass between her fingers and said, "I wanted to ask what happened at the Jack Tar. You didn't quit."

"No. I didn't quit." He wasn't sure how much he could say. "Young hoodlums looked for a couple and tore up the place. Their quote-unquote supervisors got what they wanted from the dockmaster. I assumed he'd mention my name. I cut and ran." He didn't see any point in mentioning the dock boy. "You suppose I'm entitled to know why I'm running?"

Mickey's eyes, which had been drifting around the party, locked onto Regis'. His gaze was cold and angry.

She studied him. Unquestionably in the eyes of his countrymen, he was far more than maître d' or bartender.

"Of course," she replied. "Every detail. I have the gist of it. Casey Lee and Bill own citrus groves that opioid traffickers are using and confiscating as a distribution point for their stuff. Aircraft land, move large quantities to storage in a barn owned by the groves—stuff like that. The groves are absentee owned by Bill's father. It's a perfect setup. Business goes on as usual, while something extra happens under the fruit trees, and the absentee owner never knows. Bill and Casey Lee spoiled it. Bill was the almost-victim of an attempt on his life. The assailants tried to frame Christy."

"Dear God. Dangerous friends. Who's this Charles Schneider?"

She tried to laugh, but he wasn't being funny. "I'm not sure I..."

"Perhaps your friend Burton should have used the name consistently, like when he checked into the marina in the first place."

"Regis, we had no idea there would be trouble. We came to look, then Bill spotted a kid in the lobby. He recognized him but couldn't place him, so he figured it had to be from stateside. He hopes it'll come to him."

She paused. "When we got to Marsh Harbour, we were no surprise. They were there. Mary Beth identified them, but they'd been warned. They never took their eyes off us and followed us to Whale Cay Passage. They tried to shoot us with semiautomatics, which would have..."

"Holy Mother of...! What happened?"

"Rogue wave saved our lives. We saw it in time. They didn't. Well, they did, but..."

Regis, confused, said, "They were behind you?"

"We cut north, flatsticked it behind the island. They were on autopilot. Captain Tray Robertson and a Bahamian henchman, Roosevelt Awbrey, jumped."

"Into a rage?"

"I saw it. Wild rapids, then they were under." She snapped her fingers. "Like that?"

"And their boat?"

"It kept going. I looked when we were north near Noname Cay, but there was nothing left. That seventy-five-foot Burger motor yacht was probably splattered all over the face of Whale Cay."

Regis shook his head. "Anyone else on board?"

Mickey, gazing out the French windows, said coldly, "I met him, a pig of the worst kind. He was a fat slob Miami drug dealer, selling epidemic-causing, addictive, hideous, prescription only at best stuff. He was a Columbian hood. We know about him."

"We?"

"I...we. We know he was their boss. Maybe he didn't drive the boat and didn't know how to shut down the autopilot. His name was Hector Caraja. I was introduced to him at the Conch Inn, in the dining room. Bill and I had dinner. They came over to the table and made introductions all around. Nothing to it, right?"

Regis, studying her face, topped off her wine glass and poured himself one before touching his glass to hers. "You're quite a woman, Young Lady." He drank half his glass, while she sipped.

She tried to smile. "My turn."

He stood tall, chin high, eyes straight ahead. "At your service, Madame."

"It ain't *madame,* Regis."

"A blessing for all males."

"Friends forever."

He added. "And coagents without boundaries in the crusade against crime."

"Could we make that collaborators?"

They touched glasses again.

She placed her hand on his arm. "We'd have been clay pigeons out there without your note. Thanks. Sorry to mess things up for you. Will the Jack Tar survive?" She kissed his cheek.

"Not the Jack Tar we know." He touched his cheek and prepared to say something, but she was already across the foyer, heading toward the ladies' room.

CHAPTER FOURTEEN
THE WINDOWLESS NIGHT

Balance achieved led to balance sustained. Quality was never relaxed. Standard Operating Procedure, SOP, was maintained regardless, all with a stiff upper lip. That was Bluff House.

Casually past nine o'clock, guests strolled into a candlelit dining room. Six tables for four filled it, set with linens, crystal, and silver. Small loaves of Bahamian bread steamed beside the flickering candles. In the kitchen, the island-girl cooks swayed with grace and poise, as they prepared. Perfect filets broiled, ovens shimmered, and deep-fry baskets gurgled. The chopping block in the center of the kitchen was covered with sliced and chopped vegetables, and, at the far end, Hostess Kitty folded her prized Caesar salad in an oversized wooden bowl.

Even so, with the hurricane clawing ever closer, stoicism withered, and tension became the main ingredient.

The back door stood open during reprieves from the squalls, but the screen door was closed. It made a constant racket, rattling, swinging open, hanging there, and slamming, as the night winds rumbled. There was a rhythm to it.

When it blew open for what was the last time, because it didn't close again, the cooks stopped short and looked up. Kitty noticed and looked with them, almost jumping with surprise.

"Dear God, Boy."

He stood under the rear porch light, dripping on the stoop. The top of his head and shoulders were lit, with his face in shadow.

"Boy, you frightened me half to death. Whatever are you doing out there?" She reached to pull him inside, but he recoiled. "Come in, Young Man. Nobody's gonna hurt you."

He took a tentative step forward, and the screen door whacked closed behind him.

"Let me get you something."

His teeth chattered in clenched jaws. His hair and clothes were shiny wet, his face dry, and he smacked parched lips.

"Ruthy, run and get a towel," Kitty said. "Martha, fruit juice, please. Quickly. When did you eat or drink last, Boy?"

He slurred words from his cottony mouth. "The radio. Use the radio."

"Why of course. Certainly, but I want you to drink first."

Martha handed her a milkshake-size glass of orange juice. Kitty pressed it into the boy's hands.

He guzzled, spilled some, and flicked at his soggy shirt. "I must use your VHF now, Ma'am, please."

Kitty, taking the boy's arm, guided him toward the foyer. As she passed Martha, she whispered, "Get Regis."

Regis appeared from the lounge where they were cleaning up after cocktails. He stepped into the darkened hallway opposite the kitchen, which was darker than usual, because the workers outside were boarding up the windows. He stood beside the VHF by the door leading to the deck.

The figure approached tentatively, assisted by Kitty, both of them backlit from the kitchen. It took Regis a moment to recognize the boy from his posture and the shape of his head. He'd seen that silhouette all day through the binoculars. Without letting on, he asked, "May I be of service, Sir?"

The boy made no show of recognition. "I'd like to use the radio, please."

Regis gestured to the mic. "It's on."

Kitty, turning back to the kitchen, said, "He's terribly dehydrated, Regis."

"I'm not surprised. Go ahead, Young Man. Make your call. I hope, whoever it is, they aren't offshore tonight."

The boy stood without picking up the mic, obviously wanting privacy. Regis stepped around the corner into the lounge.

The boy grabbed the mic and pushed the button. *"Enchantress! Enchantress!* Come back!"

The sound rang through the foyer into the dining room. At one table for four, knives and forks, some with food attached, dropped to the plates or clattered to the floor.

Bill stood slowly. His wine glass slipped but landed perfectly, not spilling a drop. No one noticed.

"*Enchantress! Enchantress!* This is Bluff House. Come back."

Bill ran from the dining room down the foyer. He was about to smash into the figure using the radio when Regis stepped up, grabbed him, and shook him.

"My good man, Mr. Burton, what in the world…?"

"Who are you?" Bill struggled, trying to get around Regis. "Why are you calling that boat? Who are you?"

"May I suggest we restrain ourselves," Regis said. "Please."

Bill regained enough control to say, "*Enchantress* was hit by a tidal wave at Whale Cay Passage. She won't return anybody's call."

Regis released his grip.

The boy looked up at Bill. Silvery light from the kitchen reflected off his Black face.

Bill felt it all come together. *The boy from the Jack Tar was the boy at Palm Beach International Airport. He stowed the luggage in the Cadillac and saluted Captain Robertson until out of sight. He's the one at the hotel at West End before he disappeared.*

"We looked at each other in the Jack Tar lobby," Bill said flatly.

"Yes, Sir," Regis agreed. "He followed me all the way this afternoon. He does odd jobs for the *Enchantress'* Captain, or he did. This is Roosevelt Awbrey's son."

"Mr. Burton, Sir?" the boy asked. "About *Enchantress?* What about the crew?" He was almost begging.

Bill shook his head. "No. The girls saw Robertson and another man jump off at the east end of Whale Cay. They said they never saw them surface."

The boy leaned back, his head against the door, as if trying to accept the news. "Sir, you saw my father jump? My family will want to know. Please. You were outbound, near the east end?"

"East Hill Point."

The boy nodded, digesting the news. His hand moved behind him, slowly turning the doorknob. He looked first at Bill, then at Regis. Suddenly, a thought struck him, and he whispered, "The blue light."

The door whipped open in an instant, and he leaped out into the stinging rain. He shot across the deck, over the rail, and disappeared into the wet night.

Regis and Bill rushed after him. Regis was halfway over the rail when Bill stopped him.

The boy disappeared down the slope into the darkness, leaving only the sound of crashing underbrush.

"Let him go," Bill said. "He can't go far."

Bill turned, shrugged, and walked through the small crowd gathered in the doorway before continuing toward the clubhouse.

Regis remained where he was, trying to see through the rain that the floodlights turned into a shimmering wall. Somewhere, a limb snapped and rolled down the hill through the thickets.

His gaze followed the sound, then he glimpsed something and squinted. It was on the shore, a tiny light flickering like a match. It moved over the water swiftly heading south. In a few seconds, gray fuzz closed around it and pinched it out.

It would be the same seven miles for Winny that it had been for the Bertram, but it was different, because the gray monster awaited.

Gradually, Bluff House's dining room cleared. The host suggested they gather in the morning and be prepared and packed to move into the hillside shelter in the event hurricane winds exceeded 125 miles an hour. His point was twofold and gained the desired results by clearing the dining room and letting the guests know, without igniting panic, that the situation was serious.

Only the Bertram crew remained at their table. Nubs of candles flickered in an otherwise dark room.

Pearce appeared again in a yellow foul-weather jacket and carrying two more. "I'm on my way down to the harbor. Perhaps you boys should join me and check the boat. I'm sure I could use a hand."

He winked at the women, as the men stood and hustled into the jackets before following him from the foyer.

The women heard the front door open, and a loud buzz went through the foyer that rattled the picture frames of famous guests on the walls and left them askew. Then the door slammed, caught by the wind.

They sat in silence in the flickering candlelight. The two stubs dribbled on the tablecloth.

Mickey sipped her cold coffee several times. Finally, she set it down, shielded the tablecloth, and blew out the candle. When she moved to the second one, Mary Beth said, "Wait. I..."

"Just leave the luggage where it is, Mary Beth. Everything will be fine."

"Mickey?"

"Look, you've been fretting about it all evening. All through dinner, you looked at me, then at Bill, studying us and pushing your food around. Let me straighten you out. Yes, he's a winner. He proved that when he jumped out of an airplane and survived. It was a miracle. He'll be a big man in Florida, sooner than he thinks, but he isn't *my* man, so go for it. I don't want you sleeping with me, and I have every intention of corralling Mr. Casey Lee Christy, so it doesn't leave you much choice. Leave the luggage where it is."

She blew out the last candle. In the pitch black of the windowless room, she asked, "Shall we go, Miss School Teacher?"

Mary Beth didn't move. Sitting in the dark, she twisted a napkin in her lap. She said shakily, trying to be firm, "I can't do this. You brought him here. You chartered the boat, arranged everything, risked your life. Surely, you..."

"Me? He jumped at the suggestion. He's scared, Mary Beth, but he's mad, too. Once he thought about it, he would've walked on water to get here. I just added a little comfort." Mickey leaned forward with her eyes closed despite the darkness. Quietly willing herself to say the words, she added, "I'm just a paid hand lady, a hired hand, and not a very good one. I keep making friends and lovers out of clients, and that's a no-no. You aren't supposed to be friends and certainly not lovers with...the johns."

She walked away, leaving Mary Beth in the dark.

Outside, the wind moaned hysterically, buzzing against the building. The roof soffits trapped the air, making it whistle mournfully before it raced over the peaks and down the other side across Abaco Sound.

Mary Beth heard the door to the deck open, the wind wail, and the door close, as Mickey found her way through the dark. The storm shutters resumed their increasingly angry rattle.

Mary Beth Holly was no less afraid of the dark than when she was a little girl, alone in her room, tucked into bed on stormy nights. When lightning flashed on the ceiling, she drew the covers up to her chin and squeezed her eyes shut. Thunder rolled, and she tried to think beyond her fear.

Years later and far from home, it finally worked. She put her head back and closed her eyes in the darkness of the strange room and situation and surprised herself with a smile. *Whatever else you may be, you're one hell of an actress, Mickey,* she thought.

Out on the slippery deck, after leaving the clubhouse, the door with the brass number five on it came up fast and at a strange angle, as the wind and rain buffeted her. Running up the deck, she raced along the path. Nearly blinded by stinging rain, shielding her face with her arm, she grabbed the doorknob to save her balance and bolted through the door into the room.

The towel around Bill's waist blew off when the door opened, and it lay on the floor around his feet. He was so shocked, he couldn't move, as was she.

"I got wet down at the boat," he said.

Her eyes clicked shut but not before they traveled down his muscular body. She whirled back to the door and hurled it shut with flat hands.

Bill quickly picked up the towel and rewrapped it around his waist. "I thought I'd take a shower. I suggest we both..."

She turned back to him, her hands on her hips as if shocked and offended at the suggestion of a joint shower.

"I mean," he said quickly, "we should each take one. It might be our last chance for a few days."

She was neither shocked or offended. Seeing he was covered up again, she strode past him to her open suitcase on the bed to find something to wear. Her two-piece bikini was on top, and she lifted the fabric as if contemplating it. "Excellent idea, Captain."

She couldn't believe her behavior. With total nonchalance, she stripped off her wet dinner clothes, a sleeveless green cocktail shift, and hung it on a hanger before placing it on the clothes rack opposite the bathroom. As she stepped to the bathroom door, she unsnapped her bra. Flipping it over her shoulder, she asked, "Coming, Mr. Burton?"

Mary Beth had never been in a shower with a man in her life.

She turned on the water and stepped out of her panties, letting the water run through her hair and down her back. It was only warm, but it still felt good. She felt herself shaking.

"The hot water heaters are probably turned off," bill said, right behind her.

She amazed herself again by asking, "Soap my back?"

As he reached over her shoulder to cock the shower head down and send water over her face and chest, she felt his chest hair touch her back. He took a bar of white soap and lathered her, first in the middle of her back in circles, spreading suds up to her shoulders and neck, kneading between the delicate bones, then on to her buttocks, between them and the soft inner sides and back of her thighs.

She reached up and held onto the pipe of the showerhead, her body taut. His arms wrapped around her, exploring her flat stomach and breasts. His fingertips drew circles on her extended nipples.

"Turn around," he whispered.

They made love almost all night. They heard the storm becoming increasingly angry just beyond the walls, but the constant droning became part of their madness.

First, they shoved the suitcases to the floor and peeled back all but the clean bottom sheet. The first time, they crudely devoured each other. Trembling, aching with desire, tiny bubbles at the corners of her mouth, she felt him hover over her and pulled him into her with her legs. It was frantic at first. He was hard and went deep. He knew he might have hurt her, but she wanted so much so fast.

Finally, they settled into a rhythm that was easy, slow and meaningful.

When it was nearly dawn, they lay on their backs under a sheet with the pillows fluffed under their heads, and talked. Mary Beth wanted to know where she stood.

"Lover," she cooed, "what's your relationship with Mickey?"

"Friends, I guess."

"Do you believe she's a prostitute?"

"I think when she wants someone to think she is, she is."

"I knew that. Are you in love with her?"

"No."

"Is she in love with you?"

"I think she's been looking for her Marlboro Man, and I think she found him."

"That's a combination."

"Ironic, isn't it? One, they meet. Two, they fall in love. Three, a hurricane."

CHAPTER FIFTEEN
CAUGHT ON A BARBED HOOK: CAMELLIA

By noon, under the roof trusses at Bluff House, they felt the vibrations and could almost see the roaring nightmare. A body of wind twice the size of Florida, unobstructed over an area of 100,000 square miles, lay against the Abacos, like the earth's crust pushing against a continental fault. The wind gauge stood at sixty-eight miles per hour and continued climbing while they watched in awe, silent hysteria slowly consuming all.

One scrap of good news was that Camellia showed a slight northerly change in track. Officials conjectured she'd follow the Gulf Stream up the low-pressure trough that skirted the west side of the Bermuda High, which might spare the Abacos from the hurricane eye. Even so, the full fury of the northwestern quadrant, the most vicious, followed by the southwestern, appeared unavoidable.

Maximum sustained winds were estimated at 180 miles per hour, a strong Category 5.

Bluff House evacuated, with Regis leading the way. The path, etched into the steep west face of Big Bluff, descended from the redwood deck down to an elevation fifty feet above sea level and dead-ended at the shelter entrance. The shelter had been painstakingly dynamited and carved from the rock face.

Regis put his shoulder to the low-slung, heavy plank door and pushed. The lights spilled over the path as if it were night. Standing in the entrance, he held the door open.

They filed through the five-and-a-half-foot-tall by five-feet-wide opening. The uniformly short Abaconians, seven generations of intermarrying after their anti-Royalist ancestors settled the Out Islands, marched straight in, while the U.S.-born had to duck. There were forty people in all, including a dozen newcomers who straggled in from the town, nearby resorts, and beachfronts, all drenched and blown dizzy.

The interior, twenty-by-sixty feet of reinforced concrete with slab floor and anchored with driven steel pilings, was buried deep in the rock formation. The rear third was screened off and divided between a mess room and sickbay. There were cots, clean pillows and cases, sheets and blankets, all of which Regis lugged down in advance, plus an odd assortment of furniture—couches, chairs, pool chairs, lounges, and folding tables. He'd been going up and down the path almost all night. The air conditioner was on, and power was available as long as the main generator at Bluff House lasted.

After Regis took a head count, he turned to face the group, amazed at the many ways people faced trepidation. A few women wept quietly into handkerchiefs. Some sat sullen or dazed. Most hadn't slept.

One or two people packed and unpacked their little cluster of belongings, drawing satchels and bags close to make little piles as if sheltering their possessions.

One man bitched constantly but inaudibly through clenched jaws, as if he'd been served cold coffee.

Near the rear, one group stood in a circle and drank. The women laughed when their men did, but the men laughed too deeply, their belt buckles jumping when they forced themselves to laugh while their eyes were glazed.

Some read or pretended to. One man, wearing a coat and tie, read a two-day-old newspaper. He looked up with an ashen face, as if his predicament hadn't dawned on him until he read about it.

Regis counted him, the last of the group. Pearce Cody, their host, normally ruddy, bouncy, and upbeat, stood grim-faced near the rear, comforting people. He glanced repeatedly toward the open door where Regis remained on station. He wanted to order the door closed, but he worried about stragglers. There was also the fact that when the air pressure dropped like a rock outside, it would skyrocket inside and blow the door off its hinges and into Abaco Sound, exposing them to the elements. The wind would gut the place with a thousand tiny tornadoes.

There was no shortage of evidence. Buildings looked reasonably intact on the outside. When the wind got in, though, it created lift and used the ceilings for wings, totally demolishing the interior in vicious whirls.

The door would have to be closed at some point, but not yet. The barometer was still diving, closing in on twenty-nine inches.

Peripheral squalls passed, replaced by a solid, dark, gunmetal slab low across the Abaco sky, so mammoth it appeared stationary except for the churning, swirling underside. The belly scraped westward across the landfall and drafted rolls of smoke back into itself, inhaling not only flying debris but also hundreds of confused birds. The creatures, hurled into the shrieking wind, flapped wildly out of control and simply evaporated.

Regis watched the relentless approach. There was no longer any living thing in sight except trees. He felt like a lost blind man near the edge of a cliff, trying to sense it.

The air outside the shelter door, the moisture sucked from it, burned hot and dry. The sound was either bellowing and omnipresent overhead, or it was missing entirely. If he dropped a stone or coin, he doubted he'd hear it strike the ground.

His ears popped as if after a deep dive. Fear went through him, as when he'd been a child.

"Young Man? Mr. Regis?" an elderly, well-dressed widow type asked with a practiced smile, clearing her throat. "If I might ask, have you actually been through a hurricane?"

He tried to stand tall and look confident, as he said, "Oh, yes. I..." He had no idea what to say next, even though he'd been through it before.

In two decades in the Abacos, he'd been through twelve hurricanes, mostly glancing blows. Three found the northern Bahamas directly in their path. Only Hurricane Donna in '60 and terrible, billion-dollar Betsy in '65 were killers. With limited communication and nowhere to run, hurricanes took entire families, settlements, and remembrances.

"There was one when I was a boy," he said. "It was a storm in the late fifties. Few had names back then."

The storm roared over his home in heavily populated Dunmore Town on Harbour Island, Eleuthera. The totally exposed barrier island faced the Atlantic Ocean and measured less than half a mile east to west. The hurricane flattened it.

"I was young, and there were few stories, but I remember hearing..."

He knew there were hundreds of untold stories, but there hadn't been many left to tell them, and few remembered. He had noted in himself and others that the hurricane experience never registered in memory, because no one could fully comprehend it. They didn't remember exactly what they'd been through or the describable details, caught on a hook's barb, surrounded by ocean. The only words that people used were *horrible, devastating, terrifying,* and *frightening.*

"Well, Young Man. Was it quite frightening?"

"Maybe a little frightening, yes." He stopped, realizing he was using the same words everyone else did, the same pathetic meaningless clichés.

The dowager looked up, searching his face. Regis tried to be reassuring. "These days, our mariners and citizens are better educated, have better technology, better forewarning systems, better..." The sentence died.

Reading his expression, she brought a handkerchief to her gaping mouth before scurrying away.

He realized he couldn't have told her about Donna or Betsy, either.

"Regis," Pearce said, "let's close it up."

Together, they swung the heavy door closed, and Regis slid the bolt home.

CHAPTER SIXTEEN
MICKEY'S ISLAND

It lasted forty-two hours.

They listened, absorbed, and imagined every decibel and nuance of Camellia. They heard each howl, roar, whine, blast, scream, wailed fear, hysterical sob, whimper, and angry outburst. They endured pacing feet and wringing hands, every suggestion, explanation and opinion.

Rounds of vomiting, urination, and bowel movements brought odors to every nostril. In their various ways, they visualized and lived it far beyond anything they would ever see or remember or care to remember, yet they would never be able to recall it fully.

The time of day became indefinable in the shelter, except on wristwatches. People looked at their watches for a while, then quit. Others eventually stopped asking. The hours strung out and ran together like puddled oil. The long night crawled past as if comatose, to become unseen morning, then unknown afternoon, then two long days.

The rumbling outside dissipated so slowly, no one noticed. A slow-born silence strung out across the cloistered hours, until, by instinct, they sensed it, and their eyes sought contact with each other. People fidgeted, stood, and drifted forward in uneasy anticipation.

Then came the shock as blades of blazing light outlined all four edges of the door, as Regis opened it.

Framed in the doorway, a rarefied, clear, spatial-blue sky held a glowing sun above sparkling Abaco Sound.

They burst from the shelter like schoolchildren freed by the bell, blinking and shielding their dilated eyes. The more exhilarated tumbled down the hill, flopping in stony shallows. Twosomes danced their way up the path. Those parting to make way for them clapped out a rhythm for the dancers. Other came out hesitantly and dropped to their knees.

Bill carried Mary Beth piggybank, as they charged up the hill, Regis right behind them. Mickey and Casey Lee lingered to let the crowd go first.

At the top of the hill, Kitty and Pearce Cody climbed the steps to the wood deck with their eyes closed, holding hands. When they looked their jaws dropped open.

"It's still here!" they shouted

The eye of Camellia passed east of the Abacos. She raked Green Turtle with 240 linear miles of hurricane force, then angled northward to follow the Gulf Stream northeasterly, offshore of the U.S. Atlantic Coast. Florida's East Coast escaped.

At Bluff House, trees were down. The pool had become a giant planter. The shed roof was askew. Small boats enwrapped trees. The Wind Speed Indicator, frozen when the pole snapped, read 120 MPH, with gusts up to 150.

In the harbor, small boats were submerged or thrown on shore. The string of four mooring buoys, including the Bertram, were afloat, though down a foot in their sterns.

Casey took Mickey in his arms. Her mouth opened and welcomed his tongue. When they parted, she said quietly, "Let's take a walk. There's a little island, my island."

They grabbed a blanket from the shelter and moved down the bank to the shore, then waded north until the coast turned into a rocky cove. They climbed over ancient coral, a craggy promontory that formed the south arm of the cove, and stood on a slab at the water's edge.

Out in the cove was Mickey's Island. Fifty yards long, with a beautiful stand of coconut palms, it was encircled by white beach and looked like a postcard.

"I like it," Casey Lee said.

She smiled at him. "I like it, too. Come on." She pulled off her T-shirt and worked on her bra. "Leave the clothes on the rocks."

He looked at her and swallowed. It wasn't that he'd never seen a naked woman, but none were like Mickey, and none had been in sunlight. She tipped her head back and pushed her black hair off her neck and shoulders. Her body glistened with sweat over her even tan, except for bikini marks.

She waded in.

"I'm not much of a swimmer," he said.

"We can walk most of the way. Keep the blanket dry, if you can. Come on."

She eased forward in the waist-deep water and breast-stroked. He watched her legs open and close under the surface.

She rolled on her back, reaching with one arm, then the other. Water bubbled between her breasts. She stopped in the shallow of the island beach and lay propped on her elbows.

He followed, lifting his knees as he walked. The water grew deeper where she'd been swimming, until, with a breath, he went under, as did the blanket.

He didn't pop up for several seconds. Suddenly, he surfaced between her legs in the shallows.

Mickey threw back her head and laughed. "I thought you couldn't swim."

"My teacher had big jaws and a long tail, but he was great underwater. He could eat you up, Woman."

She refused to believe any of the stories he told in the shelter about his youth, though she visualized a boy in a dark, swampy pool, crisscrossing underwater before exploding onto a grassy bank.

She studied that so-called Cracker boy, who made so much sense, was so filled with knowledge, but remained close to his instincts. He was beautiful and wild, though still tender. She wondered where he drew the line and if he could kill.

Her hands went behind his neck and pulled him to her in the shallows. He kissed her navel, her nipples, between her breasts, her throat.

The base of her spine touched bottom, and she came up to meet him, groped, and found him. He penetrated her slowly, then entered her mouth with his tongue. The warm salt water, flowing over and around them like light lubricant, made their skin squeak. Their fingertips stroked ears, necks, and ribs, and their bellies rubbed. Awash in an undulating bed, two diverse creatures found each other.

The late-afternoon sun eased low over Great Abaco Island. The Sound sparkled greenish blue. On the far side, in the deep water of the big island's coast, white clouds gingerly tested the breeze.

The two spread out the blanket and lay on their stomachs. Finally, Casey Lee propped himself up on one elbow so he could stroke her back and look at her. His fingertip moved up and down the curve of her back. He never tired of touching her.

"I love you," he said.

Mickey turned her face away, shaking her head slowly, her hair flicking back and forth across her neck.

He was stunned. "You don't have any feelings for me?"

She propped herself up on one elbow, her eyes wet. "Of course I do. I was in love with you the second we met on the Bertram, but I don't want any secrets between us. Right now, I..."

"What secrets?"

Glaring at him, she blurted, "Hasn't anyone told you, Boy, I'm a prostitute?"

"No, Mickey. Nobody has. Nobody has to tell me what you are, either." He wiped her tears away with his thumb. "Don't underestimate these Cracker boys, Lady. I do have some questions about you, but that ain't one of 'em."

"What?"

He lay on his back with his arms out. "You comin' here?"

Down on the dock in the twilight, Bill said, "This southern living is great. I can see why you like it, Casey Lee."

Casey Lee, ignoring the remark, dragged his partner down to the harbor while the girls freshened up. He wanted to talk, so he leaned on the rail and stared out at the Bertram.

"Mickey and I will bring back the boat. You fly."

"OK," Bill said.

"Thought I'd stop in Marsh Harbour and do something about the safe-deposit box."

"The fact that it's not ours hasn't dawned on you? We ought to turn it over to..."

"Got my name on it. I think I should protect it."

"From whom, Casey Lee? They're surely dead. Our troubles are over."

"What if that one-in-ten-thousand shot they're not? In the Blue Cypress Swamp, we learned to play dead. Couldn't they pay off Basil at Barclay's Bank? Couldn't they drill it out?" He looked at Bill. "We did."

As Bill watched, tiny smirk lines gathered around Casey Lee's eyes. "Bull, you get on a plane, Boy. If there isn't one, charter it, will ya?"

Casey Lee wondered how long it would take someone to find the trail even if a safe deposit box was closed out. He had to see Cooper Hannah at the bank soon.

"Got anything in mind?" Bill asked.

Casey Lee's answer had the sincerity of an evangelist. "I tend to agree with you. We should do the intelligent thing regarding the money. I don't want it squandered, either. I think we should forgive and forget our enemies, namely Tray Robertson, my loving stepbrother, and his Bahamian friend—if they're alive."

Bill waited for the punch line.

"It has to do with something I thought of while sitting in Trent's den at the Rolling R Ranch. I was contemplating a business maneuver, what y'all would call a 'corporate restructure.' It was the same day you fell out of that airplane up in Yankee land."

The following morning was almost all good-byes, except for Casey Lee and Regis. Regis helped him bring the boat alongside the dock, fuel it, top off the oil, showed him how to change filters and monitor temperature and do basic seamanship.

The two of them squatted next to the starboard engine.

"Regis, Bill and I have unexpectedly come into some money. It's in Barclay's in Marsh Harbour. We've agreed to set up a foundation called The Friends of Abaconian Children and use the money for educational assistance. We want you to run it, be the director, and administer it. What do you say?"

Regis stood and unhooked the engine hood, so they could lower it. He had a pretty good reading of Casey Lee, but Regis also recalled his other commitments. He wanted to head north and do a little official recon of Grand Cay and Walker's Cay, to see if the blue light had given another miracle or if Roosevelt Awbrey and Captain Tray Robertson were, in fact, dead. The police, and, most importantly, the Bahamian government, would want to know. If Awbrey were still alive, the first place he'd go would be back home to Grand Cay.

"We thought the first kid would be Winston Awbrey. We'd give him a scholarship and get him out of here."

Regis bit his lower lip and hid his amusement.

"Shouldn't take too much of your time," Casey Lee continued. "We'll help the kids, maybe one or two a year, make sure they get the money and then get in and *stay* in school."

Regis saw how serious Casey Lee was, yet he wanted to burst out laughing at the irony of it all. He was about to take a job dispensing funds that should have already been confiscated by the Bahamian authorities. He had to admit that, despite what he would guardedly call a rather strong relationship with his government, his chances of being caught in a compromising situation were slim. The job would be more rewarding than being a one-time maître d' at the Jack Tar or his temporary employment at Bluff House.

"I'd be honored, Mr. Christy. Why don't I run up to Grand Cay and have a talk with the boy's grandma, Roosevelt Awbrey's mama?"

"And maybe you could..."

"I'll call you by VHF or by phone back at your office. I might even have occasion to be stateside soon." He paused, holding out his hand. "Mr. Christy?"

"Mr... Regis, I'm sorry, but I don't think I ever got your last name."

"It's Willoughby, Sir, Regis Willoughby." He studied Casey Lee's face, but there was no sign that he knew the name, which made Regis smile.

CHAPTER SEVENTEEN
THE MERGER

At noon, Casey Lee and Bill crashed through the office door of Burton Groves, Inc., saying, "Lord Almighty, Penny. It's hot out there."

Penny, at her desk, excitedly waved her notepad. "You just missed a call from a marine operator. That's a first, right? She had a ship's captain on the line, of the *Abaco Treasure,* or he said he was. He wanted to relay a message from a Mr. Regis. You ready for this?"

Bill closed his eyes. "Go, Penny."

Pulling her reading glasses from her hair, she put them on. "Number one: 'Big Mama delighted re: the deal'—whatever that is. Two: Mr. Regis says that she said Roosevelt somebody and Tray Robertson had been there and were now in Florida. That's it."

Casey Lee and Bill stared at each other. Stunned, they knew the vague fear they'd been carrying with them was real.

Penny looked at Bill, then at Casey Lee, then she pushed the glasses up her nose to look closer at Bill. "Darlin', I don't believe you're quite used to the humidity. Oh, Mr. Trent Robertson called you, Casey Lee, before this. He wants you at the Rolling R right away, either or both of you if possible. He meant in a heartbeat. Believe me when I say there was a bee between the britches and the leather buggin' Mr. Trent."

"I'll call." Casey Lee disappeared into his office.

Bill gazed numbly at Penny's notes, envisioning one very special young Black boy in the dark foyer at Bluff House just before he leaped into the storm. He said something about a blue light.

Casey Lee called Arthur Wendell Ryan before calling Trent. Wendell said they'd be honored to make the bank's conference room available the following morning and assured Casey Lee they wouldn't be disturbed.

Trent Robertson reluctantly agreed to come to town.

Wendell set pencils and glasses at each place around the conference table and placed an icy pitcher of water in the center. Trent Robertson, at the head of the table, ran his hands through his white hair.

"Yes, he's home," Trent said. "He's acting mad as hell at you. He said you jeopardized his position over there. He almost had to fake his something-or-other, blow his cover or whatever, to keep you alive. I'm in the dark, but I hope you aren't. What in God's name were you doing in the Bahamas, not to mention in a hurricane?"

Bill was stone-faced. "You believe him?"

"About what?"

Bill, leaning forward, tried to speak sternly enough to get Trent's undivided attention. "Did you believe him that we almost blew his so-called cover, that we jeopardized his position with whoever—the FBI or DEA, maybe the Narcotics Bureau or the Sheriff's Department? We don't know. Do you? Does anybody?"

"Now hold your horses, Young Man..."

"Trent, what we know is that he's been skippering a yacht off and on for almost two years for a boss who's a narcotics trafficker in opioids, with probable Mafia connections. The boat carries high-powered weapons. The crew includes a known area illegal substance dealer and money launderer. The guy met with Tray and was witnessed by Mary Beth Holly. He's the biggest man you'll ever see, a Bahamian. Tray knows when the aircraft landed in our backyard. Why doesn't he blow the whistle?"

"I've explained this to you before. I was told the authorities will blow the whistle when they zero in on the top dogs."

Casey Lee sat back. "You're quite sure? You aren't skeptical anymore like you were?"

Trent looked at him, then at Bill. "Exactly what did you guys stumble onto over there?"

"There's one little item," Bill said. "It's a safe deposit box with over two million in cash, and a bank book with the record of wire transfer around the world."

Trent was floored. "You mean you broke into...?"

"We played a hunch. Somebody took advantage of a certain party. They used his name, his signature on receipts and airline tickets, and you name it. Sound familiar? I figured they might use him again to open a nice little account at a friendly local bank. I took their patsy with me, and he walked into Barclays Bank at Marsh Harbour, five hundred feet from a certain yacht, and the bank opened that safe-deposit box, and lo and behold." Bill sat back.

Casey Lee watched the older man, guessing Trent wouldn't be happy with Bill's flippancy.

"I take it you didn't stick up the bank," Trent said.

"Didn't have to. All sucker boy had to do was walk up to the window, state his name, and prove it."

"Whose name was it, damn it?"

Bill assumed Trent knew, but he wanted it spelled out. "Know anybody who ever tried to use Casey Lee Christy? How about Captain Tray? He and his friends tried to kill us and followed us to Whale Cay Passage, while we ran for a hurricane hole. They came up on our transom, and the Bahamian on the foredeck with a rifle tried to get a shot at us."

The fire in Trent's eyes slowly went out, and he looked down.

"Your son almost drowned," Bill added. "Surely he told you that?"

"No. I don't know anything."

"It was a tidal wave. They were so busy trying to blow our brains out, they never saw it. It was a monster twice the height of Wendell's bank here. We ducked behind the island just as it was breaking. Tray and the Black man jumped at the last second. We thought they were dead. Maybe they're lucky."

Trent stared at Bill.

"We figured they were on autopilot. Their boss probably never knew what hit him. I don't suppose they're very happy with us. The yacht's a total loss, and they're missing their prize bankbook and several million dollars."

Trent looked at them both. "You took it?"

"We moved it," Bill admitted.

"They know you've got it?"

Bill shrugged. "It's doubtful. They're sure it's there, but they can't get at it. There's still a safe deposit box in Casey Lee's name, but they're not signatories anymore."

Trent was silent.

Finally, Casey Lee said, "Trent, I think we should merge Rolling R Ranch with Burton Groves. How about that? It solves everything."

As the silent room became dead still, Trent seemed stupefied.

"Some time ago," Casey Lee said, "out at the ranch, you explained some of your plans regarding your affairs. It was late afternoon, the day I got word our friend here hit the asphalt airstrip in Connecticut. You recall, I'm sure. I started to ask you then if you would ever consider something, then I withdrew it. I said I'd ask you another time. Remember?"

"I remember."

"I wasn't quite prepared. You were upset, because doubts were starting to dawn about Tray. You were worried about the future of the ranch after you're gone."

"You'd be worried, too."

"Your stock in the surviving company is your only risk, one that would be diluted by 4,000 acres of prime citrus. After the merger, counting your groves, the surviving company would be one of the bigger operations in Florida. Your only worry would be who inherits your shares at the time of death. I predict, in the near future, we're looking at land values of $25,000 an acre. That comes to $150 million, Boys."

Trent, dumbfounded, absorbed what he heard. Bill assumed he'd be arguing if he disagreed.

"What in hell does this have to do with what we've been talking about?" Trent asked, sounding exasperated.

Casey Lee bet he had a motive Trent would accept. "I figured if you basically approved, you'd have some stipulations. One, that Tray be taken care of with a job. We've got one for him."

Trent shuffled in his seat, as Casey Lee continued.

"If we lock him out, he's gone, right? We don't know where he is or what he's up to. Every dark corner will mean danger for us. Sometime, some night in bed, I'll wake up with a gun barrel under my chin and someone asking for two million dollars and a little black book.

"Right now, Tray and his friends don't know how much we know. They know the safe-deposit box is there, and they think the money is there. They don't know we peeked at their little book, so they don't know we know anything.

"We go along. We offer Tray a job. Rolling R's the major player here, so it would be a top job. He'll know he's fooled us if we give that to him. He'll even come to the office, at least at first. He'll figure he's got time on his side. It'll dawn on him how smart he is, smarter than anybody, and then..."

"We make our move," Bill said.

"Or someone forces him to move," Casey Lee said. "Remember, somebody will want to know about Hector Caraja, his demise, or at least his books, along with the operation's proceeds and a million-dollar yacht."

Trent cleared his throat. "What kind of job?"

"Chairman of the Board, of course," Bill said matter-of-factly, looking right at Trent.

The silence might have lasted forever, except Arthur Wendell Ryan opened the conference room door and stuck his head in. "Excuse me, Gentlemen. We're closed. It's after seven, and I was wondering…"

"We're through, goddamn it!" Trent bellowed.

Wendell started to duck out, but Trent called him back.

"Young Man, are you president of this bank yet?"

"No, Sir."

"Stick with these two, and you will be."

CHAPTER EIGHTEEN
INNOCENT AS MARSHMALLOWS

On Friday afternoon, soon after Trent Robertson agreed to the merger, he stood at a window in his old ranch house study, looking out at the rain. The citrus crop didn't need rain. It needed a cold snap to kill fungus and bring out color.

His mind was on the money. He hoped and prayed 10,000 acres of citrus could carry the sinking cattle operation. Only a year earlier, he realized he couldn't hold out any longer. Rolling R was broke. He took out a second mortgage on the place, the first time in years, and never told the employees or anyone else that the business was failing. There was always a chance that cattle prices would revive. Retail prices weren't slipping, but the price offered on the hoof was an insult to Florida cattlemen.

He lost confidence. It was then he made a mistake, a very big one that might prove fatal.

His reflection in the windowpane stared back at him. It had always been a face of power and optimism, but that wasn't what he saw. Outside, rain droplets clung and ran down the glass, making the trees and front gates wobble disjointedly.

Everything was disjointed. His biggest worry of all was that Tray disappeared again in the middle of the night. Trent knew it was his own fault.

The merger would buy time, and things might blow over, but something that big?

He finally noticed he'd been standing at the window a long time before what he'd been staring at beyond the glass came into focus. Someone was on the road beyond the front gates.

The man was tall, rail thin, stooped, sallow, with a thin dark mustache and stringy hair combed straight back. His suit looked rumpled. He wore a white shirt with dark tie, and he kept looking up and down the road, stealing glances at the house. Finally, he put his hand on the gate.

Trent, assuming the man was lost, stepped out the front door and waved in a neighborly fashion for the man to come through the gate. "Afternoon to you. Need some help?"

The man ignored him, straining to see up and down the road, until Trent reached the gate. He looked at Trent from a face wherein the dark eyes moved, but the rest of the face held no expression.

"Looks like you're a might lost, Friend," Trent said.

Without moving his mouth, as if his teeth hurt, he said, "Acquaintance named Tray Robertson. Know where I can find him?"

Trent's heart pounded. He held his hand over the gate, hoping the man didn't notice him stiffen. "I'm Trent Robertson. Tray's my son."

The visitor didn't take his hand. "He here?"

"Not at the moment." He moved his hand farther forward. "You, Sir?"

The man looked at the hand, then at Trent. As if to get past the ceremony, he finally shook Trent's hand.

"Hector Caraja."

Trent almost yanked his hand back but caught himself. "Well, Mr. Caraja, will you come in?"

He stretched his lower lip in a negative gesture. "Tell him I was by. Got his paycheck. He drove a boat for us in the Bahamas."

"Yes, I heard. It was lost in the storm. Sorry."

The man turned and watched a car pull out of nowhere and come toward them. It stopped, the back door popped open, and the man started to get in but hesitated, turning back to Trent.

"He's holding some money for me. I'm here to get it."

"But does he know...?"

The door slammed.

"...where to find you?"

The man rolled down the window and leaned out, smiling for the first time. He tapped the driver's shoulder, and the car lurched off.

Trent turned away to avoid the flying dirt from the wheels.

On Monday morning, Bill Burton, Casey Lee Christy, Roy, the general manager of Rolling R, and two lawyers gathered around the conference table. Dick Burton telegrammed that he couldn't make it for the first stockholders' meeting, but they had his blessing.

Mary Beth Holly and Mickey Morgan-Lloyd were there as observers, and, if required at some later date, as witnesses to the Board's resolution to elect a new Chairman. Tray, of course, never showed.

Trent tried to hide how upset he was. "Well, Gentlemen." He waved to the two lawyers. "Guess we'll have to reschedule."

The lawyers stood, closed their briefcases, said good-bye, and closed the door behind them, as they left.

Trent gestured to the others to remain seated. Once the room quieted, he said, "A man came to the house Saturday, said he owed Tray captain's wages. He said Tray was holding some money for him, too. I had the feeling he wasn't talking about just a few bucks."

"Did he give a name?" Bill asked.

"Yes. That's the point. He said he was Hector Cara-whatever it is." He watched the others react with shock.

"Hector Caraja?" Mary Beth, wide-eyed, asked.

They all felt numb.

Casey Lee looked at Trent. "Ring a bell?"

Trent looked back curiously and said, "No."

"What did he look like?"

"Odd. Tall, real sickly thin, dark suit and tie, dark, thin, stringy hair, and a little mustache."

Perplexed, Mickey asked, "That's Hector Caraja?"

"They've come out with a new model," Casey Lee said flatly. "They want to know what happened to the old one, and they want their money, all two million plus. The guy Trent met is the replacement."

"Would someone tell me what's going on?" Trent asked impatiently.

"They've got Tray," Bill said.

"Since he worked for them," Casey Lee said, "they made him take them to the money at Barclays Bank, Marsh Harbour. He's probably standing in the vault beside Cooper Hannah this minute. It's Monday morning, so first things first, right? Why wait?"

"Can they get in the box?" Bill fought back panic.

"They can get in the old one. We never closed it. When Mickey and I went there after the hurricane, I told Cooper to keep it going with the same old signatures, including Tray's favorite, mine."

"But they changed the lock," Bill said.

"Cooper sent me the keys. I checked my filing cabinet. They're gone."

"Well, Jesus, Boy! Why didn't you say something?"

"It didn't matter. That box is empty, as you know. The two mil is in the box beside it, and the key for that one is in my pocket. It matters now, though. When Tray slides open that drawer in front of his new, thin friend..."

"He's dead," Bill said flatly, "unless he thinks fast. He's a good thinker. He doesn't know he hasn't been elected Chairman of the Board. I'm sure he told them he's top dog in charge of a key Florida distribution point, and their worries are over.

"Whether he's working for them or is an undercover agent, that would buy him a few days, time enough to prove he has the situation handled. If he's undercover, and they're onto him..."

Nominations were opened, seconded, and closed without discussion. Thirty seconds later, they unanimously voted Tray Robertson as the new Chairman of the Board of Directors of Burton Agri, Incorporated.

They sat in silence, staring at each other. There was nothing more to say.

"Shall we report him missing?" Mary Beth blurted. "Call the police?"

"No," Casey Lee said. "He'll show." He stood and pushed back his chair. "Let's get out of this hot box. It appears little ol' Northerner Wendell isn't familiar with the air conditioner yet."

Stepping through the bank doors to the outside, the women in the lead chatted over what a relief the cooler temperature was after the conference room.

"Nice, huh?" Bill commented.

"How nice it'll get is the question," Trent replied, looking up through live oak branches. Thin, high, altostratus clouds skimmed over the bank roof, as bright and innocent as marshmallows.

Casey Lee, the last one out, heard their remarks and paused, holding the door open. "Twenty degrees cooler than when we got here," he said, putting his fist to his ear to signal a phone call. "See ya. Gotta make a call."

The four stepped to the sidewalk, while Casey Lee went inside.

Arthur Wendell Ryan had never seen Casey Lee's gray eyes blaze like that before. "Yes, Sir, Mr. Christy. Use mine. Sit at my desk, please."

*　*　*

Penny knew full well when Casey Lee meant business, especially on the phone. His pitch went up, and he seemed to kick each word off the roof of his mouth with his tongue.

She took down his orders, then repeated them back. "The boys get down fifty stack heaters from the loft and place them outside on each side of the barn doors right now. Fill them with Bunker C oil from the fuel wagon, 500 gallons, which will empty the wagon. Push the empty wagon onto the barn floor.

"Of the remaining heaters in the loft, which is 400, place 200 on each side of the loft against the east and west walls. Call the fuel company to fill the main fuel tank, the one on tall legs outside at the east end of the barn. They'll know it. It takes 2,000 gallons of gasoline, not Bunker C. That's two-zero-zero-zero gallons today, earliest possible time."

Lastly, Casey Lee asked about the weather.

She knew the answer and rattled it off. "At six A.M. in Atlanta, it was thirty-eight degrees. The forecast is twenty-five to twenty-eight degrees overnight. Yes, Sir. I'm positive. Possible hard freeze in Central Florida tomorrow night. That's verbatim. Sir? Mr. Christy? Casey Lee?"

Casey Lee hung up and thought, *tonight.* He replaced the pure white receiver on its cradle.

CHAPTER NINETEEN
NIGHT IN THE GROVE

Bill agreed to come out to the groves to check temperatures. Apparently, Mickey called the office and asked Penny if anybody would mind if she came out, too, saying she could read a thermometer.

"I feel involved and just want to be there," she added.

Bill guessed she must have wormed the information from Casey Lee. She also indicated Regis would be there. Bill wondered why the man was stateside. It seemed that Mickey and Regis formed a bond in the Bahamas, a mutual serious concern regarding opioid trafficking in general and the mob that threatened their lives during the hurricane in particular, as well as threatening Central Florida.

Bill shared her concerns. She said her Palm Beach parents were recreational users, and she feared they were moving toward lacing heroin with fentanyl. It was fifty times stronger than straight heroin, a hundred times more than plain morphine.

Bill wasn't about to tell Casey Lee what to do. He was a good reader of predators, and he would do any crazy thing he wanted. He came straight to the office after changing out of his clothes from the bank meeting. He told Bill that any trouble would happen well before the forecast freeze, because a freeze meant lots of extra traffic in the groves. However, Casey Lee hadn't indicated what kind of trouble or any plan of action to counter it. He just said he had a hunch.

"I'll come and have a look," Bill said.

"Fine. I'm through talking, anyway."

Since Bill arrived in Florida, he saw that citrus groves in the light of day looked like any other cultivated, groomed farm crop. It was just trees instead of plants like corn, potatoes, or strawberries.

It wasn't that way at night, especially that far south. The climate was directly related that they were 27.5 degrees north latitude, where the tropics began. In the summer, the area was tropical, while in winter, it was temperate.

That night would be a typical grove night, though no night under those canopies was truly typical. It was moonlit above the canopy and hot, vaporous, wet, and without shadow below.

Night in the groves turned tree trunks into dark stone monoliths and returned flora and fauna to their primeval ways. The law of the jungle was the rule. It was the time of predator and prey, hissing, screeching, split-second violence and eerie silence.

Dusk came quickly across the flatland. The near darkness hid creatures' faces, making them motionless, as they waited for their eyes to dilate, so the blindness of low sun would surrender to keen night vision.

Casey Lee was one of them.

He squatted for over an hour, an Ithaca shotgun across his knees, hidden in the dark shadows of the towering Australian Pines, a species of fern that grew into trees. They ran perpendicularly away from each end of the equipment barn. The trees, first taking root there from seeds blown across the Gulf Stream from the Bahamas on the prevailing southeasterly, were once thought to provide good wind blocks, and they lined almost every grove in the area.

The air that night was westerly and so light that blades of tall grass under the trees rasped audibly when they rubbed against each other. Casey Lee preferred enough breeze to rattle the trees and provide cover for hunter or prey, whichever he became, should he inadvertently drag a boot heel, give in to scratch an itch, or grab a whining insect in his fist. The groves were usually breathless after sundown.

He squatted Indian fashion to allow exercise. A man could rise and stretch, free up his circulation, look around, and drop back down without moving his feet and risking snapping a dry twig. It was a Seminole trick, based on the theory that no man could stand in one place for any length of time, especially if afraid. When a man eventually moved, he surrendered.

Casey Lee rose slowly, moonlight striking his face, to flex his legs and let his eyes pierce the night across the nursery grove. The partial grove, 100 yards wide between the rows of tall pines, looked like a dark banner of broad stripes and dark furrows, rising convex mounds and concave swales, which made for good drainage.

Rows of tiny, metallic-looking citrus budlings, with protective white boots shining, dotted the elevated stripes. Across the way, a parallel row of pines stood shadowed. To the south, the long corridor the grove formed eventually melted into a distant black tree line.

Without definition and paved by moon glow, it looked like an airstrip.

By three o'clock that afternoon, the men had fifty heaters in front of the barn and fueled with Bunker C. They correctly assumed it was a head start on the potential weather. They left the fuel wagon bone dry and pushed back into the center of the barn, as requested. The rest of the stack heaters were lined up nicely on both sides of the loft.

Casey Lee nodded his approval and told the boys to go home for the day. If temps dropped below minimum, they'd be working 'round the clock the next few nights. Penny had it right about the weather.

The fuel truck arrived to fill the tall gravity storage tank on long, vertical legs adjacent to the barn. The driver, not the usual man, shied away from customary chatter. His wide-brimmed hat pulled low against the sun, he went to work.

Casey Lee, on the second floor, heard the fuel truck finally leave. He ran an irrigation drip line hose along the inside base of both side walls and the back wall, camouflaging it where it wasn't hidden behind the stack heaters, mainly along the back wall, using tall, old-fashioned picking ladders no one used anymore. Tall citrus trees were a thing of the past, giving way to the economically more efficient chopped and channeled look. After poking out a knot in the wood along the east wall, he ran a drip line outside.

He hauled the gravity tank hose fifty feet off the reel and tied the nozzle to a twenty-five-foot length of rope, then he hurled the rope up through the open loft doors onto the loft floor. Once up on the loft himself, he hauled up the nozzle end of the fuel fill hose and went to work.

He filled eighty of the four hundred stack heaters in the loft, one gallon each. The boys set them two hundred to a side in twenty rows by ten columns, leaving the center of the loft open, so the come-along and access to the doors was clear. He filled every heater in the fifth and sixth columns, two columns of twenty, forty each side, making eighty gallons total. The remaining stack heaters were intentionally left empty, should someone think he smelled fumes and become curious.

Next, he closed the loft doors, dropped down the ladder, and started on the empty fuel wagon, five hundred gallons.

In the dark, he shut off the lever at the gravity tank, exchanged the nozzle for connector, and connected the fill hose from the tank to the drip line that hung from the loft. Lastly, he snapped shut the padlock on the barn doors.

It was nine o'clock. The hazy moon high over the trees was poised to begin its slow slide into the western horizon. Bill would be somewhere near the nursery grove beyond the far stand of pines.

At ten o'clock, Casey Lee stood in the pines, waiting and listening, the Ithaca against the tree trunk that hid him. He squatted and closed his eyes, because there was nothing to see. Listening to the night, he pictured the grove. He pushed his hearing to the far south, off to his right, where the grove met the black tree line at right angles, then along the trees and the nothingness above. Silence throbbed behind his eyes and rang in his ears.

At eleven o'clock, he heard something like an insect that wasn't anywhere near him. Shooting to his feet, he stared into the darkness toward the southeast. A faint buzz came and went faintly, then intermittently, like stalling. Between heartbeats, the sound was gone for a few seconds, as if blown away. In the south, he heard an engine accelerate, like a plane using hard feathering. He blinked profusely and stared into two distant grayish narrow plumes rising over the tree line.

Damn, he thought. *It's down.*

Tiny specks of light flared from the ground, as multiple flashlights came on in a north-south row that resembled landing lights. That meant there were advance people already on the ground, but he saw and heard nothing.

The lights blew away. In seconds that felt like hours, a plane came at him like a charging monster, the dark side facing him, rolling toward the barn without a single light on. It was less than two hundred yards away.

At one hundred yards, it squealed its brakes and feathered one engine, spinning slowly clockwise and cutting a half circle swath though the rows, kicking up baby citrus plants like tumbleweeds. The pilot shut down. In a soft flutter, the night became silent again.

He could barely distinguish the plane in the dying moon glow. It looked bigger with its light color against the Australian pines behind it. It was a twin-engine, probably the same one that landed there recently.

A vehicle he hadn't seen earlier, most likely driven by someone who gathered up the flashlights after the landing, ran forward in a furrow through the plane's settling dust trail. It swung around the plane, stopped, and backed to the fuselage on the side opposite Casey Lee, the moonlit side. It appeared to be a white delivery truck.

Doors opened. He heard lumber being horsed around on the truck, then dropped, probably a pallet they planned to use. The plane's cargo door opened just ahead of the tail. Two men, possibly the truck driver and pilot, began shuffling armloads of large packages from the plane, stacking them in the truck. Casey Lee saw their moving forms occasionally when they stepped in and out of shadow. One, the truck driver, appeared older and labored more than the other man. He had a shuffling, almost-familiar gait, and he stumbled. The interior of the rear of the truck was hidden in the dark.

Two more men moved from the truck and crossed Casey Lee's field of vision, moving toward the barn. One was a huge man with a jet-black silhouette against the blue-black trees. The other was Tray Robertson, with his characteristic strut, posture, light Stetson, and a hip-length coat, probably the brown sheepskin Casey Lee so admired.

Standing in the footprints he made over two hours earlier, Casey Lee studied the hundred yards of darkness out to the plane.

Dim flashlights came on near the truck, then went out. He heard metal rattling, then keys. That would be Tray opening the barn door. The door slid aside on its track. A rectangle of dim light popped on in the doorway.

A flashlight blinked its beam toward the truck. The truck's door opened and closed, and the flashlight beam hit a third figure, another man, drawing a path to the barn. Light bounced on and off the figure.

Casey Lee saw he was tall, stick-like, and hunched, wearing a dark suit, his street shoes grating on the sandy ground -- the new Hector Caraja.

All three men went inside. A few seconds later, the light went out.

Casey Lee counted, timing their steps, as he visualized them groping, walking, through the barn, up the ladder, pushing open the hatch to the loft, and stepping onto the plank floor. He heard the come-along slide forward on its overhead beam, the hook dragging across the floor. The loft doors opened. Flashlights flickered inside the loft doorway.

A high, thin, accented voice barked sharply, and the huge, black silhouette leaned out and started to yell to the truck, only to be quickly hushed. The big man must be the Bahamian, Roosevelt Awbrey.

The truck engine started. Casey Lee was ready to step forward, but he set his foot back down in its place. The truck pulled in front of the building and backed to the open loft doors. The driver went to the rear and left the truck idling poorly, the engine knocking.

Casey Lee used the noise to cover him. In a half-crouch, he picked his way along the tall pines until he could dart behind the end of the barn. In the shadows, he leaned his cheek against the cool, damp, barn wood, inched to the corner, and chanced a peek toward the entrance.

The truck quit.

Casey Lee froze in the instant silence.

Overhead, the come-along motor clicked on and groaned. The hook lowered. The truck driver clipped it to the lift tackle and eased the pallet from the truck. In a few seconds, it started up.

Casey Lee guessed it weighed 500-800 pounds of stacked, wrapped packages and might have included a quarter-ton pill press, to make powder into pills. It could be raw fentanyl from China via Mexico via Miami.

They slid the load into the loft. As it disappeared, the doors swung shut, probably to allow the men to turn on their lights.

The driver, his face hidden under a wide-brimmed straw hat, climbed into the van and drove off toward the east without headlights. He found the trail winding through the wooded area as if he practiced it often.

Casey Lee wondered how long it took to break down bulk packages into individual packets or tiny pill bottles. No doubt another truck, a different make, model, and color, with different plates, would show up for the pickup.

He weighed that against how long it would take them to smell the fumes or see or hear liquid moving over the floors. Pressed flat against the barn door, he tried not to breathe.

There was no sound but muffled voices and the loft floor creaking occasionally.

Out of nowhere, the silent black night in front of him exploded in noise. There was no fire or flash, but his eardrums rocked, and the concussion slammed the back of his head against the door. The shock almost stopped his heart. Wind hit him, and grit splattered against the barn.

The plane revved and coasted a couple of times, then slowly faded. Darker than the sky, it lifted off. The sound of the departing plane was gone before he could move. Trembling, he inhaled and exhaled as hard as he must to recover, wondering if he cried out without knowing it.

He slipped around the door and inside the barn. In the pitch black, he groped toward the fuel wagon, found it, and touched the stopcock. He twisted it open carefully to avoid a splash. A thin stream hit the floor and began to spread. He paced ten steps away and reached in his pocket for Penny's pearl-covered Zippo. He flicked it but never saw the flame.

The blow caught him cleanly on the back of the head and brought him down. Someone plucked the Zippo from his hand. He had a split-second glimpse of an older face, but the message never had time to reach his brain.

The assailant dragged Casey Lee's limp body outside and left it propped up. As if he rehearsed every aspect of Casey Lee's plan, the man returned to the barn, set the lighter on the floor well beyond where Casey Lee intended, and lit it.

He struggled to lever Casey Lee's body over one shoulder and hurried down the center of the nursery grove until he was out of breath. He dumped the body like a sack on the shoulder of a furrow a hundred yards from the barn. He even remembered the Ithaca and grabbed it, setting it in place beside the limp man.

Once he was done, the man walked awkwardly across the grove and disappeared through the wooded area toward the dirt road.

A few minutes later, a weak, pitiful sound came from Casey Lee. He moved slowly. "Shee-it," he moaned.

His jaw hurt from slamming to the floor, and he felt a sticky gouge on the back of his head. He forced himself to wake up.

He raised his head to see the barn in front of him. Just as his eyes focused on it, it changed.

Fumes spreading across the barn floor ignited with an insidious grunt and left it swathed in swirling orange. The concussion imploded, and trees and the ground shuddered. Another brutal shockwave came, and the loft doors blew open to slam against the outer walls. The second floor erupted in fire.

Casey Lee watched black, flaming silhouettes struggle to find a way from the scalding bath that washed over their hair and faces, backs and hands. It looked as if they were dancing.

Tray Robertson stood in the loft doorway with an automatic weapon, as flames grew up his back. He fired wildly into the grove. Rounds popped in the dirt directly in front of Casey Lee. He groped for the Ithaca, found it, rolled to a prone position with the butt to his shoulder, and waited.

Suddenly, the symmetry of diamondback rattlesnake skin was all he saw. Trent Robertson's expensive boot shoved the shotgun into the dirt.

Casey Lee whirled and looked up at Trent's face, bronzed by the fire. A hunting rifle hung from the crook of his arm.

"Trent?"

"Sorry, Son. This is a chore I can't shirk."

"What the hell?"

"It's all my doing. I'll undo it my way." He stepped back, turned to the barn, and raised the rifle to his shoulder. The barrel bobbed and weaved, as he tried to find his shot.

"No!" Casey Lee shouted. "It'll kill you!"

"I should've stopped this a long time ago."

It was too late. As they stared, Tray Robertson was engulfed. He teetered on the doorway edge of the loft, then fell back into flames before his father could fire. Trent saw his son's automatic weapon fuse itself to his belly, barrel up, firing slower and slower until it stopped.

The Bahamian, part molten yellow, part charred ashes, hunched his broiling shoulders and waved his arms violently, as if trying to fly out through flame. He disintegrated into curled layers like burning newspaper.

The so-called Hector Caraja, with his dry-twig physique, apparently never took a step after the fire exploded.

Casey Lee and Trent watched in awe, while flickering orange reflected on their faces as the night erupted into daylight. A thousand jagged veins of white soared into the night. Trapped, expanding fumes in the empty fuel wagon found the tank's weak seam and blew the first-floor walls out in mushrooms of flame and cartwheeling lumber. In a chain reaction, eighty stack heaters, with 160 gallons of fuel, went in unison, blowing the roof off. The loft floor collapsed, an undulating, molten yellow ball under it.

The adjacent, near-empty tall main storage tank on legs blew itself into sand grains and toppled into the inferno.

Casey Lee, awestruck by the intensity, got to his feet. Trent rested the rifle across his forearm.

Both watched, mesmerized.

Finally, Trent said, "That's one hell of a fireworks you planned, Son." He turned toward him. "I'm sorry I couldn't let you execute it."

Casey Lee searched his stepfather's face. "You couldn't let me what?"

Trent's gaze returned to the fire. "I hired a man to do it, a local drunk who came around as an on-and-off oil tanker driver. I staked him. He took the job. Anyway, I couldn't let you do it, so I paid him."

"How the hell did you know what I was gonna do?"

"Bill overheard Penny call in your fuel order. I called him. He didn't call me. I wanted to tell him I agreed with you that they'd come around at some point. He was scared and told me. I said I'd take care of it, then I hired a guy."

"To crack my head open? Who was it?"

"You saw him. He's the driver for the bulk plant who delivered your order. Danny something or other."

The fireworks passed its climax. Blackened timbers and studs thudded and crackled on the slab, while smoke billowed from debris. Paint cans and chemical bottles exploded like tracer fire from where the little lab had been. The barn's wiring sizzled and shorted out. Blue sparks flashed, lighting it like a stage. Casey Lee and Trent were nearly deafened by the fireworks.

A vehicle entered the nursery grove near the tree line in the south and crept along the furrows without lights to come up behind them. The sedan seemed to follow the aircraft tire tracks. To the occupants, Casey Lee and Trent, backlit by the smoldering glow, looked like armed hunters taking a break.

One hundred feet from them, the car moved onto the soft loam and stopped. Headlights came on, hitting their backs. They turned, blinded by the lights, and raised their weapons.

"Casey Lee, Darlin'," a woman called, "you put that down now and take a step back."

No one moved. Car doors opened and slammed.

"Kill the headlights, please," the same voice ordered.

Four flashlights came on, their narrow beams dancing, hitting Casey Lee and Trent's faces and blinding them.

"Well, now," she said. "Everybody hold what you got." She giggled. "You don't suppose... Am I looking at two of my favorite, endangered, rare, genuine Florida Cracker cowboys?"

Stepping from the shadows into the flashing light from the smoldering ruins, she stopped with her hands on her hips. She was long-legged in Levi's and boots and wore a light shirt open at the neck.

"Aw, did we burn down our ol' bunkhouse, Casey Lee, Darlin'?"

Her three companions, flanking her, chuckled self-consciously.

Flashlight beams settled on Trent's face, and he turned to Casey Lee. "Who are these people?"

"You must be Trent Robertson," the woman said. "It's a pleasure to meet you, Mr. Robertson. I'm a friend of Casey Lee's." She flicked a leather ID wallet from her back pocket and held it up. "Mickey Morgan-Lloyd, Special Agent, FBI."

She gestured to the couple on her right. "I think you know Bill Burton and Mary Beth Holly."

Mary Beth, trembling, clung to Bill. She tried to whisper the name "Trent" to him warmly, but it came out as a question.

Casey Lee, swallowing, blinked repeatedly.

Trent's gaze went to the tall Black man in the group.

"This is Inspector Regis Willoughby," Mickey added.

Casey Lee hadn't recognized him. "Regis? What are you doing over here?"

"Well, Mr. Christy, Casey Lee, I brought you some good news and some other news. Little Winny Awbrey enrolled in a fine school on Nassau and is living with his mother. I confess, beside your foundation, I have another job as Chief Inspector, Narcotics, in the Bahamas Defense Force.

"Mr. Robertson," he continued, "there was a small black bankbook in Barclays Bank in Marsh Harbour Mr. Burton asked me to look at. We noted a wire transfer to you of one million dollars a few months ago. A Mr. Ryan of your bank verified it as being deposited to your account. Would you care to comment?"

"Trent?" Casey Lee asked. "What's...?"

Mickey nodded to Regis, who stepped closer.

"I'm sorry, Mr. Robertson," she said, "but you're under arrest."

Trent sighed. "Which of all the possible charges are we talking about?"

"You're charged with conspiracy to import opioids into the United States of America. You're charged with conspiracy to commit murder in the attempt on the life of William Burton. I only wish I could bring charges against you for failing to step forward to stop your son from framing your stepson in that attempt. God hopes Casey Lee understands, Mr. Robertson."

"About what, Young Lady?"

"That murder, Sir, isn't quite the same as hunting."

Regis turned to face Trent, cuffed him, patted him down, and gestured he move toward the bureau's car, as the faint light of dawn appeared.

The four of them watched the two walk to the car and the car doors open, then they heard the sound of leg restraints being put on before the doors slammed. The car started back down its own tracks and disappeared into the dust cloud.

"Out at the road, Regis will turn the prisoner over to the sheriff's deputies. They'll handle him from there," Mickey said. "They'll Mirandize him. We can gather your cars whenever you're ready."

The barn was gone. The fire burned down to nothing but a hot slab, charred pieces, and black rubble. Somewhere in there were charred bodies.

As they watched sparks drift to join the fading stars, the dawn turned clear and cool.

Casey Lee stared at what had been the barn. He squatted on his haunches, facing where it had stood, toying distractedly with a handful of sand.

Mickey, her back to him, folded her arms as if intentionally looking south over the length of the nursery grove. "He was about to lose the Rolling R," she explained. "Something about beef, the ranching business. Hector Caraja met Tray in the Bahamas through Roosevelt Awbrey, which led to Trent, which eventually led to an offer of big-time money to set up a distribution point here in the boonies. Trent didn't want to know any of the details, but he bit.

"He sent his son to Connecticut, the intention being to see if the boy could be handled and discouraged from showing an interest in the citrus business. Tray's outrageous, arrogant plan was his own. He put you in Burton Groves as manager, so you would, quote, 'Do as you're told,' unquote. One million dollars bailed out the Rolling R. At least, that was the plan."

"I guess you must have some charges against me, too, don't you?"

She didn't answer.

"Arson? Murder?"

She didn't answer again.

"Hell, I was the one who was gonna torch the place and burn 'em all out."

Finally, without turning, she said, "We have the man who did it, Casey Lee. He made it easy. He jackknifed his tanker truck across the dirt road to stop us. When we drove up, he ran to us waving his arms. He knew everything about it—every move, how much fuel, where it was, the drip lines, and the stack heaters. He couldn't wait to confess."

"Who was it?"

She turned with her hands on her hips, fists clenched. "It doesn't matter."

"What was his name?"

Gently, pleadingly, she said, "It doesn't matter, Casey Lee. Enough. I want you to take me to our island right now. I love you. Please, take me to the island."

He let sand run through his fingers and slowly rose up in front of her. His eyes emerged from shadow.

She knew exactly what that look meant at a moment like that. He put his arms around her, the side of her face against his, and stood silently for a while.

After she made him promise to take her to the island—and to say he loved her—she told him what he wanted to know.

"His name is Daniel Christy. Your father?"

His spread hands against her back flexed. As her face leaned against his shoulder, she heard his calm breathing and special silence until he finally whispered, "Yes. Daniel Christy is my father."

CHAPTER TWENTY
THE PLAN

The newborn Florida day, with its baby-blue spotless sky and piercing sun, brought crisp coolness to the light northeast breeze. Whether the alleged approaching cold front would fizzle out or freeze the locals out, more than one thing would have changed. The hideous soulless souls and their insanely invaluable stash of filth in greasy, shiny packages of opioids hidden in the barn loft were gone. It was over.

Bill had been standing there for hours, since long before dawn. What happened to these four was so daunting, the risks and the luck, he marveled they were still alive. He stood with Mary Beth and stared at the dead fire without speaking.

The distant dare that began it all for him, initiated by his father in the family kitchen in Darien Connecticut, never mattered. Bill now understood what had been happening in Florida. Dad's silly rhetoric that night had nothing to do with the actual tragedy. It was the locals themselves who finally won.

Bill understood he had become one of them. It was likely he'd never call Darien his home again.

Standing with Mary Beth, the two of them were tearful and joyous for their friends, two incredible lovers who shared a poetic love few could ever know. The beautiful and surely infamous FBI agent, the daughter of decadent Palm Beach socialites, and the wild boy, born in the Florida swamplands, were two of the most-disparate and unlikely people to find each other in history, but they stood beside Bill and Mary Beth, touching. Mickey's soft cheek no longer pressed against Casey Lee's neck, but they were clearly one.

There was no question in Bill's mind about any of this. At least the vengeance that had haunted Casey Lee for most of his young life was expelled. It turned out that his father had actually done the boy a favor, by being absent so many years.

Trent would have every opportunity to walk the recreational yards at prison and consider his worst decision. When released, he would doubtless again seek his chair at the Board of Directors' table. Casey Lee probably wouldn't object out of sheer pragmatism. He would say every man deserved a second chance, although the Blue Cypress swamplands never gave anyone second shots.

Tray Robertson, a born cattleman, never understood the real animals among whom he was raised. He went for the easy brass ring rather than the gold ones, the cattle grazing in pastures and the fruit hanging from trees all around him.

Roosevelt Awbrey sought only self-improvement, a way to provide for his family and make his mama proud. Once he picked up the envelope with filthy money in it, though, he never had a chance. Winny would do better.

The other players in the dirty game would keep trying as long as other people let them. There would be help from the Feds, Florida's governor, members of law enforcement, and new legislation to educate the public. Some 64,000 people died of overdoses in the U.S. the previous year. Many had no idea what they were mixing. Fentanyl, the best example, was said to be fifty times stronger than heroin and one hundred times stronger than morphine. Overdosed parents were sometimes found dead in parked cars, their live children hysterical in the back seat.

Bill stood there, trying to figure out how to break the silence and put the whole situation to rest.

Mary Beth, apparently in agreement, poked his side. "Tell them the plan."

Bill smiled. Casey Lee looked at him, perplexed.

"My plan," Bill said, "is to turn this crew around as quick as we can and head east, to travel our beloved imaginary line at latitude 27.5 degrees north to where it hits the Atlantic Ocean at Vero Beach, Florida. Locals call it the 'Little City by the Sea.' There's an old, famous restaurant there, an eye-popping, nearly handmade-looking structure originally built out of driftwood without architectural plans or drawings. It has artifacts from all over, including Palm Beach, Miami Estates, and Europe. The builder, an eccentric, visionary, local pioneer named Waldo Sexton was a world traveler, collector, and entrepreneur. He stood knee deep in the breaking ocean surf and directed the construction himself, calling the place the Ocean Grill.

"Inside, it's all history. There's a mesmerizing, tranquilizing, comfortable ambiance. Mary Beth and I shared an ocean view table one night and found utter peace, like magic.

"What we plan to do when we get there is take off our shoes and walk barefoot into the shallows, stand in the water, and, well, say some pretty things to each other."

Mickey was already smiling.

Casey Lee asked, "What kinda things?"

"Oh, 'for better or worse, for richer or poorer, in sickness and in health, to love and to cherish.' Stuff like that."

Bill assumed Casey Lee would unleash his favorite expletive and say, "Shee-it." Once again, he surprised his friend.

"Attaboy, Bull," Casey Lee whispered. "Attaboy."

ACKNOWLEDGEMENTS

More than Fair Winds filled these sails; there were the navigators.

Years ago, I received editorial tips from friend, world-famous novelist, the late Elmore "Dutch" Leonard, who, on pain of secrecy, offered his secrets, free yet invaluable. To thank him again, I try to bring his discipline to my own style.

Some of the most accomplished names in the Citrus Industry allowed me into their lives, hearts and souls, some countless times. You helped me to try to understand this special place, where the tropics begin, and these true Floridians, many second, third and fourth generation, respectful of the finest place in the world to grow citrus. To be close to such people, I often felt I was witnessing life lived as a work of art, powerfully motivating. You know who you are. I can never thank you enough.

My voluntary readers gave their time and attention like dedicated crew: my speed-walking, high-seeded tennis ace, my adorable, insightful, devourer-of-novels, my daughter, Mary Kate York, read many drafts. Retired high school English teacher, Susan Lovelace, Executive Director of the prestigious, local, literary organization, the Laura Riding Jackson Foundation, brought corrections and discipline. Local book clubber, Liz Jaffee, put pasty notes on the pages. Analytical mind, great heart, columnist, radio host, Beth Walker Stewart, who gets it, lived it.

Others were living life rings: Charlie Replogle, Joey Replogle, in fact, the entire the Replogle family, owners of the legendary Vero Beach, Florida, Ocean Grill, Rose Dean, Mary Ann Simpson, Michael Simpson, all of the Ocean Grill staff. My Attorneys E. Steven Lauer and law partner-daughter Eva Lauer. Genius, savior, computer tech Mike Bristol. IT master Michael Clarke. And my financial anchors, Marion E. Fredrickson, Sandi Markowski, Brian J. Elwell and Russell G. Cappelen, Jr.

My warm thanks to the helmsmen who steered me with patience and kindness, my agent, Richard Lawrence and my publisher, Black Rose Writing.

My love and thanks, one and all.

NOTE FROM THE AUTHOR

Word-of-mouth is crucial for any author to succeed. If you enjoyed the book, please leave a review online—anywhere you are able. Even if it's just a sentence or two. It would make all the difference and would be very much appreciated.

Thanks!
Pete

ABOUT THE AUTHOR

Pete Clements is a lifetime writer and active member of the Directors Guild of America. *The Latitude* is his first novel.

Thank you so much for reading one of our **Crime Fiction** novels.
If you enjoyed the experience, please check out our recommended
title for your next great read!

Caught in a Web by Joseph Lewis

"This important, nail-biting crime thriller about MS-13 sets the
bar very high. One of the year's best thrillers."
–BEST THRILLERS

View other Black Rose Writing titles at
www.blackrosewriting.com/books and use promo code
PRINT to receive a **20% discount** when purchasing.

www.ingramcontent.com/pod-product-compliance
Lightning Source LLC
Chambersburg PA
CBHW011137100726
47898CB00009B/3020

* 9 7 8 1 6 8 4 3 3 3 9 6 7 *